Delilah Doolittle
AND THE
Canine Chorus

Patricia Guiver

BERKLEY PRIME CRIME, NEW YORK

This is a work of fiction. Names, characters, places, and incidents are either the product of the author's imagination or are used fictitiously, and any resemblance to actual persons, living or dead, business establishments, events, or locales is entirely coincidental.

DELILAH DOOLITTLE AND THE CANINE CHORUS

A Berkley Prime Crime Book / published by arrangement with the author

PRINTING HISTORY
Berkley Prime Crime edition / January 2001

The Penguin Putnam Inc. World Wide Web site address is
http://www.penguinputnam.com

ISBN: 0-425-17801-3

Berkley Prime Crime Books are published
by The Berkley Publishing Group,
a division of Penguin Putnam Inc.,
375 Hudson Street, New York, New York 10014.
The name BERKLEY PRIME CRIME and the BERKLEY PRIME CRIME
design are trademarks belonging to Penguin Putnam Inc.

PRINTED IN THE UNITED STATES OF AMERICA

10 9 8 7 6 5 4 3 2 1

Praise for
Patricia Guiver's pet detective mysteries . . .

Delilah Doolittle and the Missing Macaw

"A charming entry in the delightful pet detective series. Patricia Guiver showcases her writing skills by weaving eccentric, endearing characters into a cozy that has an Old World ambiance about it. . . . Readers who enjoy cozies or tales involving animals will relish the latest novel in this fine collection of mystery books."

—Harriet Klausner

Delilah Doolittle and the Careless Coyote

"The latest addition to Patricia Guiver's 'pet detective mystery series' is as witty and entertaining as the wonderful previous works. . . . A first rate mystery [that] will especially be enjoyed by Anglophiles and animal lovers."

—Midwest Book Review

"This story should please animal lovers and mystery lovers, especially those who like their mysteries along the lines of the 'Murder, She Wrote' series."

—Old Book Barn Gazette

Delilah Doolittle and the Purloined Pooch

"Delilah Doolittle and the Purloined Pooch may be Patricia Guiver's first mystery, but it reads like the work of a seasoned pro. Her narration flows smoothly from scene to scene. . . . Animal lovers everywhere will surely champion the first appearance of Dee Doolittle in Patricia Guiver's clever series opener."

—Mystery News

Acknowledgments

My thanks to fellow author, Dave Ciambrone, Sc.D., for sharing his expertise on toxic plants.

Thanks, also, to John Forrey, of Pedersen's Metal Detectors, in Santa Ana, California, a treasure trove of information on mining in the Southwest.

. . . And he and they together
Knelt down with angry prayers
For tamed and shabby tigers
And dancing dogs and bears . . .

—Ralph Hodgson (1871–1962)
    "The Bells of Heaven"

• 1 •
The Break-in

"THERE'S NO QUESTION about it, Watson, old girl," I said to the big red Dobie, curled alongside me on the bench seat of my Country Squire station wagon. "There's only a hundred miles between Surf City and San Diego, but as far as Evie and I are concerned, we live in two different worlds."

Watson nestled up closer, as if to let me know there was no question about in whose world she'd rather be.

We'd spent the weekend in San Diego with Evie and were now headed home on the I-5, the Pacific Ocean in view most of the way. Evie's husband, Howard, was away on business, and she'd begged me to come and keep her from "terminal ennui," as she'd put it when she called.

"We can go shopping, and you must stay the night. That way you won't have to rush back." Then, as if anticipating my standard excuse, she'd added, "You'll bring Watson, of course."

I appreciated that. I wasn't one to inflict my dog on other people uninvited. Not that Watson wasn't the perfect lady, but being in a strange place is confusing for an animal, and accidents do happen.

Evie delighted in her show-place home, but her love

for animals was almost equal to mine, and it was only with the aid of well-paid domestic help that she was able to maintain a reasonable balance between the two passions of house and pets. Chamois, her dear little Maltese, was rarely a problem. His feet so seldom touched the ground. But recent additions, Ying and Yang, were an entirely different matter. Under Evie's indulgent tutelage, the mismarked Siamese had grown from innocent orphans into supercilious tyrants who ruled the home with paws of iron, delighting in tormenting Chamois with their mind games. Evie had adopted them in the aftermath of the Careless Coyote case—a debacle in which she had, quite uninvited, chosen to involve herself. And she never let me hear the last of it.

"Now, sweetie," she'd said as she hugged me goodbye earlier that afternoon. "Promise me you'll not get into any more scrapes. I cannot constantly be coming to your rescue. It's just too much of a strain. You must quit that silly job and give serious consideration to moving to San Diego where we can keep an eye on you."

I'd smiled sweetly and told her I'd think about it. But nothing could be further from my mind.

She was always trying to run my life, having never been able to grasp that it was necessary for me to earn my own living. The fact that my job as a pet detective, though eminently satisfying, was hardly the stuff from which fortunes were made, only added to her frustration. She had tried, repeatedly, to get me to make a career change. Or, better yet, to marry one of the succession of Really Nice Men whom she paraded before me with tiresome regularity.

"Time's winged chariot, etc., sweetie. Mustn't be

choosey," she'd said over breakfast just that morning. "I can't understand it. You used to be the sensible one at school."

That's how long we'd been friends. Since that first day we'd met at the exclusive English girls' school where she had been a boarder, I a day student on a scholarship. We'd remained close through the years. Then, when we'd come to America on an extended holiday, she'd had the good sense to meet, fall in love with, and marry Howard, a wealthy Texas oilman. Things had not turned out so auspiciously in my case. I had married and been widowed in rather quick succession.

Fortunately there was no time right then to dwell on that sad episode. The Surf City off-ramp was coming up fast, and I had to concentrate on my driving. Watson stood up and stretched, alerted by the timing of the turn signals that we were nearing home. I shared her anticipation, and looked forward to a nice cup of tea.

"WATSON. WAIT!"

As soon as I'd let her out of the car she'd gone romping up the porch steps, eager to get inside for a nice rest on the cool, kitchen tile.

But the front door was already open, the lock broken, and the remains of the stained-glass insert in pieces on the step.

Watson stopped in mid-stride and sent a puzzled look in my direction. Catching up to her, I took a firm grip on her collar and entered the house cautiously, aware even as I stepped around the broken glass that I first ought to have gone next door to call 9-1-1. The intruder might still be inside.

"Is everything all right?" a voice called across the pink and white oleander hedge. "I thought I heard break-ing glass during the night."

It was Posey Brightman, my neighbour. Nosey Posey, I called her. She had been a friend of my late husband, Roger. We'd got off on the wrong foot when I first moved in with him. I hadn't seen much of her in the last year or so. She'd rented out her house and moved to the Bay area shortly after Roger's death. Now she was back, for good apparently. Though we seldom spoke, I was willing to bet my best teapot that she knew a lot more about Roger's mysterious background than I did.

I turned to face her as she continued, "I looked out late last night and saw a man leaving. I thought he was a friend of yours. I didn't realize you were gone. Oth-erwise, I would've called the police."

There was an edge to her voice that implied a certain criticism of my visitors. But perhaps she could be for-given in view of the odd characters who did occasionally show up on my doorstep—Tiptoe Tony and Slippery Sam to name but two. To say nothing of the visits, more frequent of late, from one of Surf City's finest, Detective Jack Mallory.

Perhaps I should call him now. But no. His beat was homicide, and I certainly didn't want him thinking that I would call on him in every emergency, however close our friendship had grown.

I asked Posey if she would go ahead and make the 9-1-1 call for me. Then, secure in the knowledge that the intruder had left, though not without some apprehension about what I might find, I stepped from the small entry hall into the sitting room.

My heart sank. Every sofa cushion had been ripped open. A cherished antique sherry glass, lovingly carried all the way from England, smashed to smithereens. Great Aunt Nell's knitted afghan lay in a gritty bundle among the broken potted plants, the dirt and leaves ground into the carpet. The carpet itself pulled up at the corners, exposing torn padding and bare boards. I retrieved a framed photo of Evie and myself with our school hockey team, wondering as I wiped off the dirt and replaced the expensive silver frame on the end table, why the burglar hadn't stolen it.

Other questions quickly followed. Who could have done this? And why? What if I'd been home? Would I be alive to tell the tale? Fear turned to anger that someone would take it upon himself to invade the sanctity of my home and destroy my things.

In the course of my pet detective investigations I had found myself in some sticky situations, but never before had I felt so personally violated.

Happily, Dolly, the cockatiel, was still secure in her cage. She gave a little shake when I entered the kitchen, ruffling her feathers as she settled back down onto her perch. Her bright black eyes gave the impression of having observed something out of the ordinary, but she remained close-beaked about what it might have been.

Watson padded behind me into the kitchen and immediately set about scoffing up the kibble that lay scattered across the floor.

Through the kitchen window I could see Hobo, the three-legged ginger feral cat, sunning himself on the back porch. I doubted the break-in had bothered him. He was a tough old chap. He'd lost that leg to a steel-jaw trap, but he managed very well as a tripod. I'd found another of those bloody traps on the wetlands a few days earlier. Now it was in my car, carefully boxed, ready to be handed in to the local Fish & Game office next time I was in the neighbourhood.

Having survived the invasion unscathed, Hobo was now scoping out the birdbath—no doubt with mayhem of his own in mind.

Stepping carefully around a mud of sugar, flour, milk, and melted lemon sherbert in front of the refrigerator, I made my way to the bathroom. There I found my Yardley bath salts—a gift from Evie—dumped into the tub; the top of the toilet tank on the floor.

In the den, bookcases and the filing cabinet were up-ended, the contents scattered. A rainbow of lost-and-found pet posters spread across the carpet. I picked up my Monks of New Skete *How to Be Your Dog's Best Friend*, the spine broken, pages torn. I had been reading about "insee" and the importance of cultivating moments of quiet communication between canine and human.

"Well, we'll have to put that project on hold for a bit," I said to Watson as she followed me into the bedroom, where I gazed in resignation at torn pillows, the upturned mattress, and emptied closets.

"THIS KIND OF thing, it's routine this time of year," said the young police officer who responded to Posey's 9-1-1 call. "You've got your transients, your out-of-towners. School's out, and you've got your kids with too much time on their hands getting into trouble." He looked no more than a kid himself, certainly too young to be entrusted with such an important job. "Get your lock fixed, and keep the doors and windows bolted.

"And take care of this immediately," he said, pointing to the gaping hole where my stained-glass pelican insert had been. I'd loved that pelican. I had splurged on it at an outdoor art festival in Laguna Beach. And had never regretted the impulse until that moment.

He handed me a form. "Fill this out, and let us know if anything is missing."

I had some serious tidying up to do before I could tell him that. A cup of tea being the first priority, I started in the kitchen. Fortunately, although the tea caddy had been overturned, the teabags were enclosed in paper envelopes and had come to no harm.

While I waited for the kettle to boil I called the locksmith. By the time I'd finished my second cup of tea he'd arrived in one of those fully equipped mobile units and, with the American efficiency so admired by the rest of the world, soon had a new deadbolt installed.

"Here, you'll need this for insurance," he said, handing me a receipt.

Insurance. That was a laugh. The door, the carpet, and the stained glass combined wouldn't meet my high deductible. What with home owner's, car, earthquake, and flood, I was insured against every calamity save not having enough of the ready to pay the premiums.

Finally I could put it off no longer and set about the dreary task of restoring my house to order. I worked my way through one room after another, picking up and putting down as I went.

It was evening before I got to the bedroom. I was attempting to pull the mattress back onto the bed when a man's voice called through the screen door.

"Delilah. Are you there?"

2

Mallory

IT WAS MALLORY. Though we had advanced to the stage of calling each other by our first names, I avoided doing so whenever possible and still couldn't bring myself to think of him as "Jack." If I'd had to give a reason it would have to be because I was not ready to acknowledge the intimacy that first names conveyed, reluctant to embrace the democratic American habit of addressing everyone, even the most casual acquaintance, by their first name.

"Blast," I thought. After working for several hours I must look a bit of a ragbag. I took a hasty glance at myself in the dressing-table mirror in the irrational hope of a sudden transformation.

But why should I care if Mallory saw me in old sweats? In fact, he'd rarely seen me anything but a mess. Like the time, during the Motley Mutts affair, when I had been dragged out of the ocean looking like an overdressed flounder. Then there was the Missing Macaw case when I'd attempted to give motorcycle chase to a fleeing felon and ended up in the hospital.

Oh, yes. Mallory and I had crossed paths and swords on more than one occasion when chance contrived to have us both working the same case. Our differences stemmed from his opinion that I was an interfering busy-body, while I regarded his refusal to listen to my theories as they related to animal behaviour as unreasonable obstinacy.

But over the ensuing months we had gradually put aside our mutual distrust and developed a grudging respect for each other's skills. We'd even had dinner a couple of times and later discovered a shared interest in bird-watching on the wetlands that lay beyond the back of my house.

Just lately I'd sensed that he would like to get closer, but I gave him no encouragement. I was quite content with the way things were, secure in my beach bungalow, my legacy from Roger—in fact, all I had left to prove I had ever been married to him—and getting a lot of satisfaction from my work. It would never make my fortune, but it offered freedom and flexibility, and, best of all, I could take my dear Watson along on the job.

"Come in if you can get in," I called as soon as I could make myself heard over Watson's barked greeting. "I'm in the back bedroom."

Odd how he should show up now, just as I was about to start on Roger's closet. I'd put it off until last because, quite honestly, it evoked too many painful memories. I had barely touched it since he'd died two years earlier.

I looked up as, preceded by a waggy-tailed Watson, Mallory entered the room.

I had to admit that his was a comforting presence. He was not quite six feet tall, a little on the heavy side, since he didn't get enough exercise. His tan was accounted for by the hours he spent out of doors bird-watching. At mid to late fifties, his thick grey hair was perhaps an inch too long, curling at his shirt collar. His blue-grey eyes were his most interesting feature, sharp, clear, didn't miss a thing, as I had learned in the past.

"I heard about the break in," he said. "Here, let me do that." He took hold of the mattress with one beefy arm and set it on the box spring.

"Now, what's next?"

Without waiting for a reply, he stooped down and picked up an overturned cardboard box.

"No, don't," I said as he started to replace papers and old photographs. But it was too late. In his hand was my marriage certificate from the Little White Chapel in Las Vegas.

He looked surprised at my reaction. He knew, of course, that I'd been married before, but I had never given him any details. Now, perhaps, with the debris of my doomed marriage scattered across the floor, it was time. He was, after all, a policeman. It was unlikely that anything here would escape his eagle eye. I might as well tell him before he drew any wrong conclusions.

"I'm all in," I said. "I was just about to take a break. Let's have a cup of tea. Or coffee, if you'd prefer. I think I might have some instant somewhere." Probably way past its pull date.

"No, tea will be fine," he said with a grin as he followed me into the kitchen. "I'd rather have a good cup of tea than a bad cup of coffee."

I didn't take offence. I had never been able to make coffee deemed drinkable by my American friends.

Mallory plopped himself down in Watson's old chair. It seemed to be his favorite despite my frequent warnings about dog hair. Anyway, he was wearing jeans in-

stead of the usual well-tailored—though always rather
sporty—suits he wore for work, so I supposed it didn't
matter. Watson certainly didn't seem to object. As soon
as she saw the tea preparations she settled down under
the kitchen table, anticipating a piece of our favourite
shortbread.

Mallory picked up the conversation where we'd left
off in the bedroom. "I'm sorry. I'd forgotten you used
to be married. It must have been hard, seeing your keep-
sakes tossed around like that."

All he knew was that Roger had died suddenly two
years earlier and that the marriage had been brief.

Over tea I told him something of how I had come to
marry in what, in hindsight, could only be described as
a fit of madness. I had been swept off my feet in a
whirlwind courtship, Roger being under the mistaken
impression, I was to discover later, that I was well-to-
do like my friend Evie, who had at that time recently
married her millionaire.

"When Evie and Howard returned from their honey-
moon, they insisted that I join them in Las Vegas, where
Howard had business to take care of," I said. "Roger
had been introduced to Howard by a mutual acquaintance from Texas. He soon insinuated himself into our
company, and the next thing I knew we were a four-
some: sharing laughs over dinner at places only Roger
knew about; enjoying top entertainers at the shows
where he seemed always to be able to get the best seats.
I realize now that he was a bit too eager to regale us
with tales of his clever investments and how much
money he was making."

I paused, embarrassed to go on. I sounded like such

a fool. Seeking a diversion I stood up and switched on the electric kettle and busied myself reheating the water for a second cup of tea.

Tall, with black curly hair, greying at the temples, laughing blue eyes, Roger had been enough to turn any woman's head, especially one recently out from England, ready to be enchanted by all things American. True to his Texas roots, he invariably wore jeans, with Western cut shirts and cowboy boots.

Mallory was looking at me as if waiting for me to speak, and I realized I had been woolgathering.

"I was thinking of his expensive cowboy boots. He owned several pairs, all made from exotic animal skins. That alone should have been enough to warn me," I said with a shudder, thinking of the alligators, lizards, and ostriches that had given their all for those elegant boots.

"Eventually, of course, it turned out that he was a con man. Fortunately, Howard made inquiries about him before investing in his schemes. But not in time to prevent me from making the biggest mistake of my life."

"Nothing about him made you suspicious?" asked Mallory.

"No," I said. "In those days I thought all crooks had broken noses, said 'dese and dose' and dressed like Al Capone. Roger looked just how I thought a wealthy American rancher ought to look."

Mallory raised his eyebrows.

"At that time my idea of Americans was largely informed by the cinema," I said in my own defence.

"When did you first suspect he wasn't on the level?"

"Unfortunately, not before the wedding. But once we came back here—he had inherited this little house from his parents, and it's certainly no mansion, nothing like I expected—there were the late night telephone calls. He would hang up quickly whenever I entered the room. And, of course, by that time Howard had tipped me off. At first I made excuses for him. There must be some explanation. Later, to explain his haphazard income and frequent trips to Las Vegas, Roger said he was taking care of investments, meeting with business contacts."

I stood up and rinsed out the teapot. "That was the first time I met Posey. When I arrived here, I mean."

"Posey?"

"The woman next door."

That bright summer evening when we had arrived, tired after the long drive from Las Vegas, Posey was in the front yard. In short shorts and cropped T-shirt showing to advantage a well-toned and well-tanned body, her streaked blonde hair cut fashionably short, from a distance she appeared to be an attractive young woman. Up close, however, a hardness in the blue eyes, and a tautness in the high cheekbones suggestive of a face-lift, put her closer to the mid-forties. Beside her I felt decidedly unglamorous with my five-foot-one frame and unruly red-brown hair.

"Roger!" She'd flung her arms around him possessively the moment he got out of the car. "Why didn't you let me know you were coming, honeybunch? I'd have called the gang over." She threw me a casual glance, and then turned back to him inquiringly.

He'd had the grace to look embarrassed. Drawing me toward him he said, "Posey, meet Delilah. Guess what? We just got married. In Vegas."

Posey had stepped back in surprise, then turned away.

She'd said very little at the time, not a word of congratulations. Later that evening I had observed the two of them in the garden. They appeared to be arguing. Posey reaching out her long slender arms to him. Roger shaking his head as if in denial and turning away.

I shrugged my shoulders, trying to dismiss the recollection of Roger's sullen mood when he'd returned to the house.

I turned back to the teacups feeling that I had told Mallory more than I had intended. I had exposed too much of my life to this man whom I had already made a conscious decision not to allow to get too close. And I was tired. All this cleaning had taken it out of me.

"I'm sorry," I said. "I think I'll pack it in for the night. Do you mind?"

Mallory looked concerned. "I don't think you should stay here by yourself."

"I'll be fine," I said. "Watson will take care of me." I patted the hard dome of the Dobie's head resting on my knee. "The officer who took the report seemed convinced that it was a casual break-in, either by young vandals or a burglar who just happened to choose my house. He didn't seem to think they'd be back."

"He's probably right. But you don't sound so sure." His intelligent eyes studied my face as if trying to read my mind. "Have you been threatened, or noticed anyone suspicious hanging around?"

"No. But I have very little of real value, and the obvious things—the television, microwave, VCR—are still here. The mess they made—I think they were looking for something specific."

"Any idea what?"

"I haven't a clue. Other than perhaps it was something of Roger's. He was the one with the secrets."

Funny. Until that moment I hadn't realized how true that was. Roger had secrets.

BEFORE HE LEFT, Mallory helped me board up the empty space in the door where my stained-glass insert had been, checked the doors and windows one last time, and said he would send a patrol car by during the night.

Tired as I was, I couldn't relax, and after Mallory had left I returned to the task of putting things back in the bedroom closet.

I really should call the Salvation Army to come and take this stuff away, I thought, eyeing with distaste a pair of ostrich skin cowboy boots. It was an indication of how insensitive Roger was to my concern for animals, that he had bought them for me. I'd never even tried them on.

I slipped my foot into one, but something prevented my toes from going all the way. Probably a wad of tissue paper, I thought. As I shook the boot out something fell onto the floor. It was a piece of paper wrapped around a small rock, rough, with bluish tinges. I picked it up and unfolded the paper. It was some kind of legal document.

Could this be what the burglar had been looking for?

I remember when Roger had given me those boots. It was the last time I ever saw him.

I returned to the kitchen and made myself another cup of tea. Then, Watson having opted for the cool tile, I settled down in her chair to study my findings and to recall the events that had led up to that moment.

♣ 3 ♣

Two Years Earlier

ROGER HAD GONE to Las Vegas on another of his mysterious business trips. It seemed like he was away more often than he was home.

Whenever I suggested I go with him, the response was always the same.

"No can do, kiddo," he'd say in the easygoing manner I'd once thought so charming but was beginning to find extremely irritating. He seemed to think he could get away with anything as long as he did it pleasantly enough. "I'll be working. People to see. No time for the casinos. You'd be bored. And you know you don't like the heat. Not good for your English complexion." He'd laughed, caressing my cheek as he spoke. "I'll be back before you know it."

I brushed his hand away in annoyance. "This is your sixth trip in as many months. You always have some reason not to take me along."

"Don't I always bring you back a present?" he said, as if that compensated for his frequent absences.

There had been too many such trips where it was inconvenient for me to accompany him. He never explained what the business was, or who these people were. But the trips would usually follow one of those late night telephone calls.

I wondered, too, if business was that brisk, why was he so concerned with the state of my finances? He was always asking about my income and savings. When I told him Howard handled what little money I had, he took the opportunity to probe for more information about Howard's business dealings, something about which I knew very little. When I told him as much he'd get resentful and act as if he thought I was holding out on him.

"Anyone would think you didn't trust me," he'd say.

I was rather afraid he was right. I feared that what I had mistaken for love was, on my part, nothing more than an infatuation with his good looks and his cowboy charm, a charm that had seemed to be in short supply since our return to Surf City. I also feared I was falling out of love with him quite as rapidly as I had fallen in. I came to this conclusion reluctantly. I had waited until I was in my fifties to get married, despite having my share of offers, and had hoped it would endure. My expectations had proved to be unrealistic, and I regretted not having got to know Roger better before diving into uncharted matrimonial seas. Maybe it was seeing Evie happily married that had encouraged me to take the plunge. But I was too used to my independence and had difficulty adjusting to sharing my life with another person, especially one whose unpredictable comings and goings left little time to develop the closeness I had anticipated. I was left with a feeling of never knowing where I stood.

Now there was no doubt in my mind that I had left it too late to marry. Before coming to America I had lived comfortably, though by no means luxuriously, on a small legacy in a flat in one of the less fashionable parts of London, office temping to pay for extras like trips with Evie.

With Roger away so much, I had to admit I missed my friend. But she was in Texas on an extended visit with Howard's family. Now, after years of being so close, all I had was the occasional phone call declaring how "absolutely vast and stark" Texas was. "Think Elizabeth Taylor and Rock Hudson in *Giant*, sweetie. That's us. All we need is that divine James Dean, and I'd be in heaven."

As for Posey, my next-door neighbour, I saw very little of her, except when Roger was around.

It was another neighbour from across the street, Ariel Ferris, who had come to my rescue, at the same time setting in motion a chain of events that was to change the course of my life.

We met for the first time when she'd stopped by my house one day while she was walking her dog, a white Pekingese, and watched as I planted a pot of pansies by the front porch.

A plumpish, motherly looking sort, with a superfine complexion and hazel green eyes, Ariel was around my own age—that mid-fifties waystation where we are wont to linger as long as possible before heading on the down ward slope toward sixty. But unlike me, keeping my hair to its natural reddish-brown with the aid of a monthly tint, she had allowed her hair to grey naturally. She wore it in a heavy pigtail, and with her long skirts, frilly blouses with low-cut necklines exposing a freckled and well-tanned neck, she put me in mind of an aging flower child.

Her voice was light and friendly. "I can let you have some geranium cuttings if you'd like," she said. "They take hold real fast and will fill in fast, too. They love the sun and thrive on neglect."

"Sounds like my kind of plant," I said, thanking her as I followed her back across the street. "In England we take up geraniums during the winter and keep them somewhere warm, like delicate orchids or convalescents." I had never seen geraniums like hers, long and spreading, with huge, brilliant red flowers.

While she took the cuttings, her little dog dug busily at a soft mound of dirt nearby.

"Now, Lulu, that's enough," she scolded as the Peke sent a shower of dirt over my feet.

"It doesn't bother me," I said, bending down to brush the dirt off Lulu's soft white coat. "I'm a confirmed animal lover." As I wiped Lulu's dirty paws, I happened to notice a black, heart-shaped birthmark on one of the little pink pads.

I soon became very fond of my new friend and her little dog. We would often go shopping or to the beach together as she showed me around the area. Southern California, where the sun shone every day, and people went barefoot even in the winter, was so different from my native moist and evergreen England. I wished I could take root as easily as the transplanted geraniums.

Then Ariel's elderly mother moved in with her, and for a while I didn't see her quite so often. "She's getting on in years, no longer able to live on her own," Ariel had explained with a sigh. "I'm afraid she's going to need a lot of attention."

Other than the usual waving to each other in our comings and goings in the neighbourhood, I hadn't seen Ariel for a couple of weeks until one afternoon she knocked on the door in a state of agitation. She was flushed, and her normally neatly braided hair was loose and dishevelled; her scooped neckline had slipped on one shoulder, exposing a bra strap.

"Why, whatever's the matter?" I asked, dreading that something had happened to her mother.

"It's Lulu. She's gone."

"She didn't run off?" I said, knowing even as I spoke that wasn't the case. Lulu was a good little dog, who never ventured beyond the boundaries of their front garden except when on a leash.

"No. Mother and I were at Knott's Berry Farm," she said, referring to a local amusement park where even the older generation could enjoy the shops and pioneer days exhibits. "We left Lulu in the car while we went in for one of their chicken lunches Mother enjoys so much. When we returned, the car was gone—stolen—and Lulu with it."

Ariel had parked in the shade of a huge oak tree and cracked the window open so that Lulu would have enough air, but not so much that she could escape. "That must be how the thief got in," she moaned.

I was almost as upset as Ariel, thinking of all the possible horrors that could have befallen poor Lulu. She might have been run over, or be cowering terrified by the side of the road, the traffic zipping past her little nose. The type of person who would steal a car wouldn't think twice about dumping a dog once it was discovered. That they might give it to someone was the best we could hope for.

Ariel was distraught. "I can't stand to think of her out there somewhere without me," she cried. "I don't know what to do."

"We must advertise," I said. "If the thieves give her away, or dump her and someone finds her, whoever has her might see the ad. And we must check the animal shelter. Was she wearing a tag?"

"Yes. She had on a little red collar with two tags, a license and a personal ID sh-shaped like a little bone," Ariel sobbed.

I gave her an awkward hug and thought about what to do next.

Thus was born my career as a pet detective. Suddenly I had a purpose in life, and I felt more energized than I had in months. We placed the ads and made daily trips to the animal shelter. A helpful kennel attendant pointed out that it was possible the car thief might travel quite a distance before he discovered the dog and put it out of the car. At the attendant's suggestion we broadened the search, placing ads in all the major newspapers throughout the Southwest. He also provided us with the locations of shelters in those areas. We made up brightly coloured flyers with two telephone numbers, mine and Ariel's, and Lulu's photo—a snapshot I'd taken of her sitting among the geraniums with a red bow in her top-knot—and mailed them off.

Ariel's car was never recovered, but over the ensuing weeks there had been several possible Lulu sightings. The most recent and most positive came a few days after Roger had left on what was to be his last Vegas trip.

I'd come home one afternoon to find a message on the answering machine to the effect that a Pekingese of

Lulu's description was performing in an animal act at a Las Vegas casino.

"You'll find out more when we know if there's a reward," said the man's voice. Unfortunately, the machine cut him off before he'd given his telephone number. That day I learned two useful lessons that were to prove invaluable as my pet detective career progressed: always offer a reward, and have an answering machine with a long incoming message tape. People tend to ramble when they start talking about animals.

To the best of Ariel's knowledge Lulu had never demonstrated the slightest interest in a theatrical career. Nevertheless, we decided the lead was worth checking out.

But at the last minute Ariel's mother took ill, and there was no way she could leave her. So I decided to go to Las Vegas by myself, take a peek at the peke, and pay Roger a surprise visit at the same time.

· 4 ·

Trouble and Strife

ROGER HAD TAKEN his Corvette, leaving me with the Ford Country Squire of dubious vintage, which he'd suggested I buy to learn on. Big and sturdy, the station wagon was unlikely to come out on the losing end of a wreck. No way was Roger going to allow me to practice on his precious 'Vette. Not that I cared much for that ostentatious car, with its bilious green paintwork, gilded with an orange-and-yellow flame on either side.

Ariel, whose insurance company had in due course replaced her stolen vehicle, would've gladly loaned me her car for the trip to Las Vegas but I wouldn't hear of it. She might have to take her mother to the hospital or need it for some other emergency. Besides, having always relied on bus or tube in England, I was far too much of a novice driver to trust myself behind the wheel of someone else's brand new motorcar.

The two-hundred-and-seventy-mile drive to Las Vegas from Surf City was straightforward enough. But with no air-conditioning, which I soon learned was far from a luxury for desert travel, I was obliged to keep the windows open to hot air and swirling dust.

There was really no speed limit on the I-15 across the Mojave, but the trip took longer than the six to seven hours I had anticipated. The wagon refused to go above sixty, and as faster cars overtook me I felt some kinship with the desert tortoises I occasionally had to slow down to avoid.

It was evening before I glimpsed the distant lights of the modern-day oasis known as Las Vegas, that place of Elvis impersonators and quickie weddings (including my own), and where taking risks was as natural as breathing, especially, as I was to learn, for opportunists like Roger.

Leaving the vast and lonely desert for the Las Vegas Strip, I felt like Dorothy approaching the Emerald City. It was hard to keep my eyes on the road in the heavy traffic, such were the fabulous and garish neon distractions on either side. Pedestrians, wide- or bleary-eyed, depending on how long they'd been there, hiked from one casino to the next seeking the big win. All eager to leave their troubles, and soon, no doubt, their hard-earned cash, behind in the themes-run-wild pagodas, pyramids, circus tents, and castles of the big hotels.

The Twilight Zone Motel, where Roger always stayed, turned out not to be the high-stakes casino adjunct I might have expected, but a rundown establishment on the far side of town. When I stopped by the office to inquire for his room number, the sallow-faced clerk made no secret that he doubted my claim to being Roger's wife.

"He don't want no female company tonight," he replied with uncalled-for insolence, his Adam's apple bobbing in a scrawny neck above a threadbare white shirt collar.

"But I'm his wife," I protested.

"Uh-huh."

Tired after the long drive and anxious to get settled, I had no patience with this jumped-up little twerp and his insinuations. "Look here. If you don't give me the number, I'll just have to knock on every door in the place until I find him."

"Okay, okay. Room 106," he said grudgingly.

It was an inauspicious beginning, and I found myself hesitating before knocking on the door, aware, suddenly, that this surprise visit might, after all, turn out to be more of a shock to the husband who, let's face it, had not been entirely open with me about his business affairs.

"Buck up, old girl," I told myself. "This is no time to lose your bottle."

I rapped sharply on the door.

"Come in. It's open," Roger's voice answered. "Just put it on the dresser." He must have thought it was a food delivery.

Peering through a haze of cigarette smoke in the dimly lit room, I saw four men playing cards. Beer bottles, ash trays, and poker chips covered the green baize table. Country music crackled from a portable radio on the dresser.

Roger, his back to the door, was raking in the chips and didn't turn around as I entered. To his left a large man of rather forbidding and swarthy aspect, his arms covered in tattoos, threw down his cards in a manner suggesting he was not having a good evening. Opposite him a short man with thin, sandy-coloured hair and a wispy moustache, stared gloomily at his own cards. He had one visible tattoo—a heart enclosing the name "Judy" on his left hand.

Only the man sitting directly opposite the door looked

up at my entrance. He was of wiry frame, with inquisitive blue eyes, a few curly grey hairs standing erratically on end on his near-bald head. He appeared much older than his companions, mid-sixties, I guessed, though his tanned face and arms and white T-shirt declaring "I'd rather be surfing" suggested a healthier lifestyle.

" 'Allo, 'allo, 'allo," he said, in an unmistakable London Cockney accent. "Pizza delivery's shaping up!"

At that, the other two men looked up, and Roger turned around, his chair scraping the worn linoleum.

"Delilah!" he said, his expression a mixture of surprise and annoyance. "What the hell are you doing here?"

Not quite the reception I'd been hoping for.

"Glad to see you, too," I said, quite put out. "Don't worry. I shan't interfere with your business." I laid heavy emphasis on the last word. "I'm here on business of my own."

I looked at the group expectantly, waiting for Roger to introduce me. But no such formality appeared to be forthcoming. So, while his companions waited with ill-concealed impatience, I explained the reason for my visit, finishing with, "And, of course, I thought it would be fun to surprise you."

I let the irony of that remark sink in before adding, "How about coming with me?"

"Hey, you're not bailing now. Give us a chance to win our money back," said the large and swarthy man in a threatening tone. Sandy-hair echoed his companion's words, "Money back."

The atmosphere grew tense. Roger looked uncomfortable. No. More than uncomfortable. He looked trapped.

As if sensing trouble, the wiry little man threw down his cards and looked directly at large-and-swarthy. "Well, Lofty, like I already told yer, this is me last hand," he said. "I got to get a breaf of air. All of you smoking like chimeneys in 'ere is making me sick." He stood up and turned to me. "You come along with me, missus. I'll show you around." He seemed in a hurry to get out of there. "Okay with you, Rog?"

Roger looked relieved. "Sure thing, Tony. Go along and keep her out of trouble."

I turned to leave, fuming that my husband would dare try to palm me off on a complete stranger.

"Wait up, hon," he said. "I've got something for you." He took his jacket from the back of his chair and went to the closet. He seemed to have a problem getting the jacket to fit on the hanger properly, and I wondered, briefly, if he'd had too much to drink. But finally having got his jacket stowed away to his satisfaction, he took out a shopping bag and handed it to me.

"Here you are. I told you I would bring you back a present. Now we have his and hers matching."

I looked inside the bag and saw to my dismay that he'd bought me a pair of ostrich-skin cowboy boots. I didn't know how to thank him. I didn't want to. They were quite frightful, and I could hardly conceal my dismay.

Fortunately, Roger was too preoccupied to notice. He tossed a set of keys in the wiry little man's direction. "Take the 'Vette. Don't want her driving around in that old heap of hers."

"But," I protested. "I don't even know this gentleman."

"Sorry, babe," my husband replied. "Delilah, meet Tony Tipton. We call him Tiptoe Tony. He's from Surf City, too. Tony, this is my wife, Delilah."

"Wife?" Tony said in surprise. "I didn't know you'd gone and found yourself a trouble and strife." I recognized this as Cockney rhyming slang for "wife."

Though I had lived in Surf City only a short while, it was long enough to have heard of Tiptoe Tony, local celebrity, senior surfing champion and, rumour had it, a small-time criminal. If Roger was mixed up in some kind of shady business, which, to judge from the look of his companions, I was beginning to suspect, then Tony Tipton, surfing championship notwithstanding, was not someone with whom I cared to develop an acquaintance.

My response was brief and to the point. "I don't need a baby-sitter, thank you very much. I'll find my own way about."

I headed out the door, slamming it behind me.

♣ 5 ♣

Dances with Dogs

TONY CAUGHT UP with me as I was putting the cowboy boots in my car.

" 'Ere. 'Ang on a tick. You won't get far on this caper of your'n without some 'elp."

I hesitated. I had no clear plan of action.

He looked at my car, covered with desert dust, with something like contempt, and rattled Roger's keys. "Come on. Let's take the Corvette. It'll be a lark."

I was in no frame of mind for larks with anyone, never mind a complete stranger, and especially not in the odious Corvette. As I still hesitated, Tony said the magic words: "It's got air-conditioning."

Though it was now evening, the heat had not abated. My T-shirt was damp and rivulets of sweat ran down the back of my neck. I nodded agreement.

"That's the ticket," the chipper little man replied. "Let's get cracking. We Brits 'ave to stick together." His eyes twinkled as he spoke, and he reminded me of an uncle of mine in England. Despite the incongruity of the situation in which I found myself—my husband playing cards while I took off on a tour of Sin City with a man I'd known for mere minutes—I felt comfortable with this fellow ex-pat and prepared to make the best of it.

While Tony drove we discussed strategy. It was sketchy at best and left plenty of room for the unexpected. We would visit showrooms known to have performing animal acts until we found one that featured dogs.

Circus Circus seemed the obvious place to start. With a theme like that they would surely have performing animals, we agreed. But not that night.

"Let's try the Mirage next," suggested Tony. "That's where Siegfried and Roy are playing."

But after looking at the photos of tigers in the lobby, I was sure that wasn't the right place, either. "I said white Pekingese, not white Siberians," I told him.

Tony insisted on visiting the bar at every casino, and, after a couple more disappointments, I began to suspect he was having me on, using the search as an excuse for a pub crawl. I was getting ready to tell him I would continue on alone, by taxi, when we came to the Big Top, where the marquee announced "The Busby Barkley Canine Chorus."

Nearing the entrance, we had to slow down for a group of circus clowns who were blocking traffic on the busy thoroughfare.

"What ho!" said Tony. "What's all this then?"

"Oh, how clever," I said. "They have performers outside as well."

"I don't think so," said Tony. "Looks more like some kind of demonstration to me."

He was right. Walking back from the car park, we found ourselves barred from the entrance by a platoon of militant clowns carrying picket signs reading ANIMAL SLAVERY and ANIMAL EXPLOITATION IS NOT ENTERTAINMENT.

A clown face thrust itself into mine. "You should be ashamed to give them your money," accused a high-pitched female voice as its owner pressed a flyer into my hand.

I silently agreed. I consider performing animal acts unnatural and demeaning. Though many trainers claimed that it was only with kindness that they could get their animals to perform, I didn't believe that was always the case. But my objection went beyond that. Animals doing tricks for human amusement was not what nature had intended. In normal circumstances, nothing would have persuaded me to attend a live animal performance of any kind. However, for the time being I had to put my sensibilities aside and focus on the main objective: Lulu retrieval.

Hotel security cleared a path for us and other visitors, and we hurried through the casino to the showroom, where people waited to catch the next performance.

The Big Top was shabbier than most hotels on the Strip, and, in an apparent attempt to attract a broader clientele, had made an effort to appeal to the entire family. Though they were not allowed to linger in the adult casino, kids had plenty to amuse them in a separate, junior area featuring video and pinball games. "Nothing like getting them started on the right track," I muttered to Tony.

We sat at a tiny cocktail table near the stage. After asking what I'd have, Tony ordered two gin and tonics. When the waitress brought them, he looked at me in anticipation, obviously expecting me to pay. Oh well, I thought, fishing in my purse for the cash, it's all in a good cause.

Keeping our voices low, we agreed we would sit through the performance to verify if indeed there was a white Pekingese performer, then make our way backstage and seize whatever advantage offered itself. In other words, in true Brit fashion we would muddle through. The sum total of the preparations I had made for this caper was the leash I had brought with me. I felt inside my purse to make sure it was still there.

There were quite a few young people in the audience, and I could tell by the enthusiastic reception they gave the opening act, an English rock 'n' roll band called the Yorkshire Terrors, that as far as they were concerned, this was the main attraction.

After several ear-splitting numbers from which no one over the age of twenty could be expected to derive satisfaction, the stage went dark and a disembodied voice boomed, "Ladies and gentlemen. Live from Hollywood, the world famous Busby Barkley Canine Chorus."

If I'd had my doubts about the "live from Hollywood" part, I was certainly in no doubt regarding the "world famous" bit. I'd never heard of them and was thankful for that. I already spent too many sleepless nights worrying about the fate of animals as it was.

To the recorded strains of "One   " from *A Chorus Line*, a Rockettes-style lineup of white and black standard poodles came on stage. Formally attired in contrasting black and white tuxes, and top hats attached with chin straps, the dogs pranced on their hind legs, their forepaws resting on the back of the dog in front of them, the leader pushing a child's scooter for balance. As the music wound down, the dogs appeared to sense the end of the performance, and one by one they descended to all fours and romped off stage in an undisciplined pack. Their precision training abandoned, the last two to exit nipped at the heels of the one ahead.

The curtain rose again to reveal a white, black, and tan Jack Russell terrier in a red tutu, a red ostrich feather boa around her neck, seated on a grand piano and howling her way through "Daddy Wouldn't Buy Me a Bow-wow." She was accompanied by a man in a black and white checked suit playing the harmonica.

The audience roared its approval, and the Jack Russell encored with a rendition of "How Much Is That Doggie in the Window?" But I wasn't amused. It was as painful to watch as to listen to.

Tony must have read my mind. "Poor little sod," he muttered, shaking his head. "Dog's only doing it because the noise 'urts 'er ears."

I warmed to this strange little man. Perhaps I had misjudged him about the pub crawl. No one with compassion for animals could be all bad.

Next we were treated to an ungainly performance by two English bulldogs in apache dancer–type striped sweaters and berets, tangoing to the strains of "Jealousy."

I was getting very fidgety, barely able to contain my annoyance. "This is so humiliating for the poor animals," I muttered. "I've a good mind to go outside and protest with the clowns."

"Don't get yourself all aerated, missus," Tony whispered back. "Stay calm. Remember why we're here."

At last the finale. Entering to the Triumphal March from "Aida," the poodle chorus was costumed in headdresses and skirts, like something from an ancient Egyptian frieze. They formed a circle that opened to reveal a gondola drawn by two golden retrievers. There, enthroned in the centre like the Queen of the Nile, was a snow-white Pekingese.

I gasped. Could this be Lulu? There was no way of telling without checking for the black birthmark on her paw. I felt again for the leash in my purse. This wasn't going to be easy.

"That must be the one," I whispered to Tony. "We'd best go backstage, find the owner, and, if it is Lulu, try to reason with them to return her."

"Reason with 'em!" Tony scoffed. "The dog's been stolen. Maybe they're the ones what did it. And even if they didn't, they've put time and money into training 'er. What makes you think they're just going to 'and 'er over?"

Thus began my initiation into the ways of the criminal world.

"I know the bloke what minds the stage door," said Tony. "He'll let us in backstage. Once we're in, I'll create a diversion while you snatch the dog."

"What kind of a diversion?"

"We'll have to improvise," he said. "Take advantage of whatever comes up."

"What if it isn't Lulu?"

"Then you've got yourself a dog. We 'ave to act fast. No putting her back and 'anging about to apologize. And no second chances, neiver. It's now or never."

It wasn't much of a plan.

"NO ADMITTANCE," SAID the burly fellow in charge of the stage door, which was wide open.

"Bob not on tonight, then?" asked Tony, nonchalantly.

"I don't know any Bob," said the guard.

"You must be new around 'ere, then," said Tony, reaching for his wallet. "Come on, mate," he wheedled. "Me and the missus 'ere, we just want to go and say 'allo to a friend. 'Im with the Jack Russell." Tony jerked his head in the direction of the man in the black and white checked suit, who seemed to be having a problem with the little terrier. Still wearing her red feather boa, she was refusing to go into her portable kennel.

"I don't know any Jack Russell, either," said the guard. "We've been told to be extra careful tonight because of the demonstrators."

Tony nodded his head in agreement. "Right. You can't be too careful with clowns," he said with mock solemnity. "I've known some rough ones in me time. Me and the missus, we was just saying as 'ow them subversives can give a place a bad name."

As he spoke, he palmed the guard a twenty dollar bill. No further words were exchanged. The man looked away, as if something had attracted his attention elsewhere, and we were in.

"I thought you said you knew him," I said as we made our way past stacks of portable cages, trainers, and yapping dogs.

"I know the likes of 'im, that's all that matters. Every man 'as 'is price."

No one paid us any attention. They were all too busy preparing for the next show. The Jack Russell was still refusing to go into her cage. The trainer would put her in, but before he could get the door latched properly, she would escape.

"There's the Pekingese," I said, grabbing Tony's arm and pointing excitedly at the dog sitting quietly in a basket against the wall, her Cleopatra-style headdress hanging on a hook above her.

"All right, all right," he said. "Keep your voice down. You want to let everyone know what we're up to? Just act casual-like while I thinks of something."

He was still thinking when a hubbub of hurried footsteps, barking dogs, and shouting people arose behind us. We turned to see a swarm of clowns invading the backstage area. Pushing people aside, they grabbed at the dogs right and left. Afraid that one of them would snatch the Pekingese before I had a chance to, I made a beeline for the basket and tried to hide her. A clown raced me to reach her first. "It's okay, I've got this one," I said, bending down to pick up the little white dog.

"Oh, no you don't," said the clown. I recognized the voice as belonging to the demonstrator who had accosted me in the parking lot. I had to think fast.

"But I'm one of you," I protested. "Came straight here from work. Didn't have time to change."

The fib was enough to make the clown hesitate. I pushed her out of the way, grabbed the Peke, and looked around for Tony.

My accomplice was having problems of his own. In apparent fright the little Jack Russell had leapt onto his shoulder. The trainer vainly blew commands on his harmonica, a strategy doomed to failure in all the racket.

"Go ahead, missus. Get out of 'ere," shouted Tony,

trying to disengage himself from the little terrier's clutches. " 'Urry up!"

Pushing me ahead of him, he hustled me out of a side door that, as luck would have it, opened onto the parking lot.

Once outside, Tony said, " 'Ere, take the keys. You'll 'ave to drive. I got me 'ands full."

Wailing sirens warned us that the police were on their way. I reluctantly got into the driver's seat, settling the bewildered Pekingese in my lap.

It was the first time I'd ever driven a stick shift. Amid Tony's shouted instructions, it took several false starts and numerous lurches back and forth, before we were finally under way.

As we drove off, I felt something tickling me behind the ear.

I turned to see the remnants of a red feather boa and the Jack Russell terrier clinging to the back of my seat. We had kidnapped not one dog, but two.

. 6 .
Full Circle

BACK AT THE Twilight Zone Motel, we found Roger's room in darkness. I knocked on the door several times, but finally gave up.

"I'll have to ask the manager to let me in," I said to Tony. "Roger will be back eventually."

But at the office we were in for another surprise.

"They checked out about an hour ago. Said they wouldn't be back," said the clerk, giving no indication that his disposition had improved in the interim. Then, obviously anticipating my question. "And, no, they didn't leave no message for Mrs. Doolittle."

His attitude was even more obnoxious than earlier now that it appeared his opinion about Roger not wanting to see me had been confirmed. He seemed convinced that my husband was avoiding me. "What'd he do, run out on you?" he said with a snide smile. "I told you he didn't want no female company tonight."

Since we had the Corvette, and my car was still in the parking lot, Roger must either have called a taxi or been given a ride by one of his companions. That he might have left on foot was highly unlikely. Cowboy boots are designed for riding, not walking.

"Well, we can't stand around 'ere all night," said Tony. "Let's go to my room and 'ave a think."

• • •

TONY'S ROOM, THOUGH just a few doors down from Roger's, was worlds apart in appearance. I noted the unrumpled bed, the overnight bag stowed neatly against the wall, clothes folded tidily on a chair, and no overflowing ashtrays or empty beer bottles. But what really caught my eye was the packet of Red Rose tea bags on the shelf by the coffee maker. I looked at it longingly.

"Fancy a cup?" said Tony, following my gaze.

"Oh, that would be lovely. I'm gasping. It's been quite a night."

"Well, it ain't over yet." He removed the coffee filter and went into the bathroom to fill the carafe with water. "What're we going to do with them there dogs of your'n."

"Excuse me," I said. "Only one of them is mine, and we're not even sure of that yet."

The dogs had remained in the car while we had looked for Roger. We then brought them into Tony's room.

"First of all," I said, "I'd better make sure I have the right dog. Not that it's going to make much difference at this point."

I bent down and beckoned to the Pekingese. "Come here, Lulu. Shake hands." The little dog, bewildered by the sudden change in her circumstances, didn't immediately respond. Had I made a big mistake? I called her again. "Lulu come here, sweetie." At that she came right up to me and offered me her paw.

I picked her up and looked carefully at her left front pad. "It's her, all right," I said with relief, showing Tony the black, heart-shaped birthmark.

In contrast to the Peke's timidity, the little Jack Russell seemed not in the least upset by the harrowing experiences of the last few hours. She was into everything, first scratching at Tony's overnight bag, then, when that didn't yield satisfactory results, picking up one of his rubber flip-flops and tossing it all around the room, placing it at Tony's feet, ready for a game.

Tony obliged by throwing the sandal across the small room for her, only to have it immediately returned for a repeat performance.

"What are we going to do with her?" I said, smiling. "We can't take her back."

"Why don't you keep her?" he said, handing me a heavy mug of steaming hot tea. I took a sip. It tasted vaguely of coffee.

"Me? I'd love to. But Roger's allergic to animals, or so he claims." I suddenly felt guilty talking to this stranger about my husband's shortcomings. I gave him a sideways glance to see how he was taking this wifely betrayal, but he seemed not to notice. He was gazing at the terrier with a somewhat wistful expression.

"What's on your mind?" I asked.

"She reminds me of a dog I used to 'ave when I was a nipper," he said. "I've always been partial to 'em— Jack Russells, that is."

He was an odd little man. I was fast reassessing my original opinion of him as a con artist with intentions to lead Roger astray. Anyone who'd go to all that trouble to help me rescue Lulu, and who now seemed to be on the verge of adopting this orphan terrier, couldn't be all bad.

"Trixie 'er name was," Tony was saying. He snapped his fingers at the terrier. "Come 'ere Trixie, let's 'ave a decko at yer pearly whites." Maybe her name was Trixie, or maybe she just was used to the snapping fingers. Whatever, she immediately ran to Tony and jumped into his arms.

"Sold!" I said. "She's yours." Tony didn't put up an argument, and I continued, "That's the dogs settled then." I took my mug into the bathroom and rinsed it. "I guess I'd better see about getting a room."

Tony looked doubtful. "Look. Why don't you go stay in one of them nice hotels on the Strip? You don't want to stick around 'ere in case them yobbos come back."

"But Roger wouldn't let any harm come to me," I protested.

"Maybe he won't be able to 'elp 'imself," he replied darkly.

"Whatever do you mean?"

"Never mind. The less you know, the better. Just take it from me that this is no place for a nice lady like yerself."

It being quite obvious that he was not about to elaborate, I took the local telephone directory from the nightstand and started to call some of the better-known hotels. Each time the answer came back "No pets."

"Why do you keep telling them you've got a dog?" said Tony. "Easy enough to smuggle that little thing in yer bag."

"I shall do no such thing. What if I got caught? I'd be worse off than I am right now."

"Dog smuggling don't seem to me to be no worse than dognapping," he said drily.

"And that's another thing. Even if they did accept dogs, I could hardly go waltzing into a hotel carrying a dog I'd stolen just a few hours ago. No, I'd best stay here. At least they allow pets. Or at least they haven't said they don't."

As soon as I was settled in my own room, I called Ariel. She was overjoyed to hear I'd found Lulu, though not so thrilled to learn that my return to Surf City might be delayed a day or two. I didn't want to leave without seeing Roger again. Promising to stay in touch, I rang off before she could ask too many questions. Questions for which I had no answers.

There was still no sign of Roger the following day, or the day after that. Feeling rather foolish, I called home to see if by chance he'd gone back there—either by plane, or hitching a ride with someone. There was no answer.

In desperation I called Posey.

"Can't find Roger?" she said, her voice dripping with sarcasm. "Maybe he's trying to avoid you. After you chased him all the way to Las Vegas, too. That's no way to keep a man," she sneered. I comforted myself by thinking that Posey was hardly an authority on how to hang on to Roger.

With an increasing sense that something had gone terribly wrong, there was nothing for it but to report Roger's disappearance to the authorities. Leaving Lulu with Tony, I drove to the nearest police station. There I once again became subject to the inexplicable vagaries of fate, where one minor detail leads to another, somewhat larger consequence, with the final upshot being totally unexpected and, in this case, quite mortifying.

The Ford was almost out of petrol, so I took the Corvette. I was becoming accustomed to the stick shift, and the garish paintwork didn't seem so out of place in Glitter Gulch.

At the police station I parked in the designated visitors' area, paying no attention to the young police officer who followed me in until, while I was waiting my turn at the information desk, he tapped me on the shoulder.

"Excuse me, ma'am. Are you the driver of the green Corvette?" He gave the registration number.

The colour might have been offensive, but I had not thought it to be criminal. "Yes, I am," I answered. "Did I park in the wrong place? I'm sorry. I thought it said visitor parking."

"May I see your driver's license, ma'am?" he said.

I fumbled in my wallet for the license, my conscience working overtime. This must be about the stolen dogs. Had someone identified the Corvette as the getaway car?

People were staring, and I was obliged to lose my place in line as the officer took me aside. He looked at the license, but instead of handing it back to me, said, "Ma'am, are you aware that the vehicle has been reported stolen?"

My heart jumped. "Stolen? There must be some mistake. That's my husband's car. Are you sure you've got the right registration number? He lent it to me the other night. And I'm here to report—"

The policeman stopped me in mid-sentence. "I'll have to ask you to come along with me, ma'am."

I was detained for several hours while a young, blond detective with gold-rimmed glasses questioned me relentlessly.

"How did you come by the car?"

"I told you, it's my husband's."

"Where is he?"

"I don't know. That's why I'm here, to report him missing. Really, this is ridiculous." I stood up and sat down again in my agitation. "Surely you don't think I'd be so foolish as to drive a stolen car right to your front door if I knew it was stolen, do you?"

"What brings you to Las Vegas?"

"I told you, to meet my husband."

"And now your husband's disappeared?"

And so it went, round and round in circles. My story sounding weaker and weaker as I explained first that the car belonged to my husband, and then that I didn't know where he was. It was as if he were a figment of my imagination. I could not help but feel ill-used.

"Is there anyone in town who can verify your story?"

"No," I lied. There was only Tony, and he was holding a couple of stolen dogs. Besides, I was fairly sure he had a criminal record of his own. Not much of a character reference.

I was left to wait in the small, airless interview room for what seemed like an interminable amount of time while the detective attempted to contact the car's supposed owner.

Eventually he returned. "Okay, Mrs. Doolittle. You're in luck. The owner has decided not to press charges. Says he's just glad to get his car back."

I still couldn't believe that Roger would be so foolish as to steal a car and was sure that there was more to this than met the eye. "May I ask the name of this gentleman?"

"No, you may not," said the detective in a mocking tone. "It's not department policy."

After that, I suppose the LVPD could hardly be blamed for not taking Roger's disappearance more seriously. It doubtless wasn't the first time they'd heard of a vanishing husband. A place of quickie marriages and equally quick divorces, Sin City must be the scene of many a husband-and-wife dispute over gambling, high living, other women, or just a change of heart. A missing husband didn't necessarily mean foul play.

But I couldn't shake the conviction that something was seriously wrong. Whatever Roger's faults—to which we could now, apparently, add Grand Theft, Auto—I didn't think that he would be so coldhearted as to take off in the middle of the night just to avoid me.

I was equally convinced that Tony knew more than he let on. He'd stuck to his story that he'd never met the other two men before that evening. But whenever I quizzed him for details, he would give me a look of injured innocence that while it didn't dispel my suspicions, did have the effect of silencing my inquiries.

He returned to Surf City the day following the police station episode, apparently more than anxious to get out of town; though he did express uneasiness at leaving me by myself. He took both dogs with him, promising to deliver Lulu to Ariel immediately upon arriving home.

According to the Las Vegas press, the Peke's kidnapping, along with that of Trixie, the bulldogs, and several of the poodles, had been blamed on the clowns. However, no charges had been filed, probably because an investigation might well have proved that many of the canine chorus had, as in Lulu's case, been acquired under questionable circumstances. This was indeed fortunate for me. If a case had been brought against the animal rights people, I would have been duty bound to confess that I had stolen Lulu, and, quite unintentionally, of course, Trixie as well.

After two weeks of waiting anxiously to hear from Roger, I had to go home. There seemed to be no point in staying any longer, and I was running out of money. So I took the advice of the police and went back to Surf City to wait for news.

Six months were to pass before it came. Then one evening I received the call I'd been both dreading and anticipating.

"Ma'am, this is Detective Brock of the Las Vegas police. I'm calling regarding your husband, Roger Doolittle."

"Have you found him?"

"We're not sure."

"What do you mean, you're not sure?"

"What's his dentist's name?"

"You mean—he's dead?" Though I had been preparing myself for bad news for months, I felt my knees give way, and I sank into a kitchen chair.

Brock said he couldn't give me anything more definite yet. A body had been found that might be Roger's. Dental records would help. They'd let me know.

A few days later my fears were realized when the detective called again and confirmed that it was indeed Roger's body that had been discovered in the desert about twenty miles out of town.

They were sorry, but they couldn't tell me what had happened. Cause of death was not apparent.

"Why ever not?" I demanded.

Brock sounded uncomfortable, no doubt wanting to

spare my feelings. "There wasn't much to go on. The body's badly decomposed. It's been out there, unburied, for several months."

"How did he get there, do you suppose?" I asked.

"We don't know, ma'am."

"How did you come to find him?" I pressed. I had to know.

He told me that circling vultures had led a group of BLM geologists to the remote spot in Red Rock Canyon, a rugged area of sandstone cliffs and valleys popular with hikers and rock climbers.

A few weeks later he sent me Roger's wallet. A hiker had found it along the trail leading to the canyon.

There had been the usual inquiries, but with so few leads to go on, the case had never been solved. The motel clerk confirmed that Roger had left the Twilight Zone Motel about eleven o'clock that night, and there the trail went cold.

I WAS BROUGHT back to the present by Watson nuzzling my hand to remind me she needed to go outside before we went to bed. I poured my cold tea down the sink and opened the back door for her. Breathing deeply of the cool night sea air, I tried to clear my head of that trip down memory lane.

Here it was, two years later, and just when I was beginning to put the whole miserable business behind me, the break-in and my discovery of the cowboy boots had brought it all back.

I knew instinctively that the burglary had something

to do with Roger's business in Las Vegas. Knew, too, that the burglar had been looking for the document I held in my hand.

Had Roger been killed because of it?

❖ 7 ❖
Back to the Present . . .

IF I'D NEEDED any further convincing, it came the morning after the break-in. I was cleaning up the broken glass on my porch, and there among the shards I found a matchbook cover. About to sweep it away with the rest of the trash, I noticed it bore the shooting star logo of the Twilight Zone Motel. I picked it up and discovered on the inside cover a serial number of some kind written in barely legible pencil. I slipped it into my pocket to study later.

I was brushing the remaining glass slivers into the dust pan when Tony's vintage woody station wagon pulled into the driveway. The wetsuit and surfboard still dripping seawater and hanging out of the rear window indicated he had come directly from the beach. He was wearing his customary uniform of white T-shirt and black OP-brand shorts. Sand clung to his rubber flip-flops. Though in his seventies, he was as spry as some men twenty years his junior. He was of hardy British stock having been raised to perfect health, he liked to say with his customary twinkle, on a diet of chip sandwiches and bread and dripping.

Trixie, the Jack Russell terrier, having retired from her career as a canine chanteuse, was by this time a familiar guest at my house. She was first out of the car, and made a beeline for the kitchen, where I guessed she would soon be nose-down in Watson's kibble bowl. Watson never seemed to mind. Like me, she regarded these occasional visits by the Tiptons as an unavoidable fact of life.

"What 'appened 'ere, then?" said Tony, surveying the boards in the front door where the stained-glass insert had been.

I told him about the break-in. "Come in. I've got something to show you. Fancy a cup of tea?" I continued as he followed me into the house.

"Wouldn't say no," he replied cheerily.

In the kitchen Trixie and Watson were playing tug of war with a bunch of Roger's old socks I had knotted together when I was clearing up the previous evening. Of all her toys, a sock rope has always been Watson's favourite.

We sat at the kitchen table while waiting for the kettle to boil. Tony looked at the still-partially cleaned up mess and shook his head.

"Whoever done you over did a proper job. They must've bin looking for something partic'lar. Is anything missing?"

"Not so far as I can tell. The obvious things are still here. The television, my few bits of jewelry, credit cards."

The electric kettle clicked off. I poured the boiling water over four Red Rose teabags (Tony liked his tea strong) in my large Brown Betty teapot and slipped Aunt Nell's purple and yellow knitted teacosy over the pot.

Tony watched while I set out two cups and saucers

and fetched a tin of Walker's shortbread from the cupboard, then said, " 'Ere, what was you going to show me?"

I took the matchbook from my pocket. "This look familiar?"

He nodded, turning the matchbook over in his gnarled hand. "Where did it come from?"

"Found it on the doorstep a few minutes ago."

I watched him carefully as he opened up the matchbook and looked inside. Perhaps I was expecting some sign of recognition. "Any idea what those numbers mean?" I asked.

He shook his head. If the numbers rang a bell, he gave nothing away. "Blowed if I know. 'Aven't a clue."

"That's not all." I went to the kitchen drawer and took out the document and the rock. "Last night while I was sorting through Roger's things, I found this. It appears to be the deed to some property in Nevada."

Tony looked at the document in surprise. "You *found* it?" This time I thought there was a sign of recognition. But Tony was an expert at dissembling, and I still couldn't be sure enough to comment on it. "Where?" he demanded.

"It was stuck in the toe of one of those dreadful cowboy boots Roger gave me the last night we saw him."

I poured the tea, first putting milk in each cup. "Is that rock what I think it is? Silver?"

He bounced the rock lightly in his hand. "I don't know nothing about that kind of stuff. What makes you think so?"

"I looked it up in my field guide." I handed him his cup. "You never did tell me what was going on when I interrupted your card game that night. The night we rescued Lulu and Trixie."

At the sound of her name, Trixie dropped her end of the sock rope and came to my side, anticipating a treat. I broke off a piece of the shortbread I'd been about to dip into my tea and gave it to her. Watson, the sock rope still in her mouth, joined her. She wanted a treat, too, but in order to take it she had to drop the rope. At which point Trixie, having gobbled down her treat, picked up the rope and romped off, inviting Watson to chase her.

Tony took advantage of the interruption to avoid answering me. I didn't press the point, saying instead, "I think I should go back to Las Vegas and find out what this is all about. If this property belonged to Roger, then it's likely that I'm entitled to it. God knows, I could do with an infusion of funds."

The pet detective business barely broke even. I'd never had a head for figures and had purchased a pocket calculator to help simplify balancing my checkbook, but had soon realized that only a drastic reduction in expenditure or dramatic increase in income would make that task any easier.

One of the mysteries of Roger's death had been that he'd left no liquid assets. No indication whatsoever of how he'd supported himself. I could locate no bank account, no savings or investments, or life insurance. No dollars stuffed in the mattress. All that was left was the forty-four dollars in the wallet the police had returned to me. Other than the house, and that heavily mortgaged, he had left me nothing but a mystery. A mystery that I was going to have to solve—if not for the sake of my bank account, then certainly for my peace of mind.

Tony placed two heaping teaspoons of sugar in his tea and stirred thoughtfully. "I don't know, luv. Those blokes were dangerous. Look what 'appened to Roger."

Suddenly I remembered how anxious Tony had seemed to leave the card game that night. Had he been scared? "You think he was murdered, don't you? And that those men at the card game had something to do with it?"

"Well, 'e didn't die in 'is sleep, did he?" Tony shook his head. "What's your man Mallory got to say about the break-in?"

I bristled at his implication. "He's not my man."

Tony rolled his eyes in disbelief.

"But anyway, he's inclined to think that it was random. Told me to be sure to lock the doors and windows in the future. Of course, he doesn't know about all this yet." I indicated the deed, the rock, and the matchbook cover on the table. "I didn't discover them until after he had left yesterday."

"You gonna tell 'im?"

"No, I'm not. It's got nothing to do with him. And for once he won't be able to tell me to stay out of his business."

"You won't 'arf cop it when he finds out."

"Oh, I don't doubt he'll be mad, but I've already made up my mind. I don't have to inform him of my every move."

"Nah then, luv. Be reasonable. It's for your own good."

"My good is my financial well-being," I retorted. "And I have every intention of taking care of it."

Brave words. But I didn't want Mallory involved in

my personal affairs, and I certainly didn't want to argue about it with Tony.

I changed the subject. "What brought you by today, anyway?"

In the two years that had passed since our Las Vegas escapade, Tony and I had become better acquainted and had even worked together on a couple of missing pet cases, but he seldom came by just for a chat. He must want something.

He shifted uncomfortably in his chair. It wasn't like him to be at a loss for words. He leaned down and picked up Trixie, who immediately began licking his face with enthusiasm.

He gently pushed the little terrier's nose away. "Give over, luv," he said.

I could tell he was playing for time. "Come on," I said. "Out with it."

"Well, it's like this 'ere. I was wondering if you could take care of Trix for a few days."

"Is that all? From the look on your face I thought you had something serious going on." I held the teapot over his cup. "More tea?" He nodded, and I continued as I poured, "I'd like to help out, but as I told you, I'm going out of town myself. I'm leaving for Las Vegas tomorrow."

I walked him to the door. Posey was sunning herself in her front yard. "Hi, Tony," she called.

"I didn't know you two knew each other," I said to him.

He grinned. "All the girls know me. It's one of the 'azards of being so good looking."

I gave him a playful shove. "You wish."

All joking aside, knowing there had been a connection between Roger and Posey, and now here was evidence of another between Posey and Tony, I wondered whether the acquaintance was quite that casual.

· 8 ·

On the Road Again

"Why can't you wait for a couple of weeks? I'm due some vacation time and I can come with you." Mallory ran a hand through his thick, grey hair in frustration. "In the meantime, you could make inquiries from here."

"Because school starts in a fortnight," I said tartly.

"So what?"

"So that's when I'll start to get busy again. People come home from vacation and find that their dog or cat has disappeared during their absence. They don't always realize that their pets are not going to take kindly to the change in routine, and if their caretakers aren't careful, the animals are likely to make a run for it."

As Tony had predicted, Mallory had been more than a little put out to hear I was off to Las Vegas. Even more so when, attempting to justify my abrupt departure, I told him about my discovery in the boot. He'd used every argument he could think of to dissuade me, beginning with dismissing the trip as a wild goose chase and working up to calling it downright dangerous. But my mind was made up. While generally of a compliant nature, I do have a stubborn streak; usually manifested in an unwillingness to accept any advice offered "for my own good."

"Watson, don't be a pest, sweetie," I chided as she

bounced up to Mallory and invited him to a tug-of-war with the sock rope. But he good-naturedly picked up the loose end, damp and chewed though it was, and gave it a tug. I sighed. It was hard to argue with someone who was being so nice.

"Now you've done it." I laughed. "She'll never give you any peace now." I tried to distract Watson by rattling her food dish, but she ignored me. "This really is the best time for me to go," I continued, almost apologetically, faced with his obvious concern. "Before I get stuck with another case."

Fortunately, or not, depending on how one looked at it, there was nothing outstanding. The frantic July fourth rush was behind us when pets, left alone in backyards, are panicked by fireworks and run off in fright. It's the busiest day of the year for animal shelters.

Finally, with a shrug of his shoulders and a plea that I stay in touch, Mallory left, and I returned to preparing for my trip.

It wasn't quite as straightforward as simply packing a bag and leaving. I had dependents to consider. Watson would be going with me, but Dolly-bird and Hobo had to be cared for. Ariel, who usually helped out on such occasions, was out of town, and Tony, my backup, was off on pursuits of his own. I could have boarded Dolly at the vet's, but Hobo presented a different kind of problem. Wild and independent though he was, he'd become used to dining on my back porch, and if the regular meals stopped, he might wander off. I wouldn't want to lose track of him. Ours was an odd relationship: we kept each other at arm's length, but there was a mutual respect, and I didn't want to disappoint him.

There was nothing for it. I would have to ask Posey to help me out.

I was a little hesitant about approaching her. We had never been on exactly friendly terms, and, since Roger's death, which she had hinted at on more than one occasion as being somehow my fault, she had been even more distant. So I was surprised, but nevertheless relieved, when she readily agreed to come in each day to check on Dolly-bird and put fresh food and water on the back porch for Hobo.

Probably wants to have a good nose around, I thought uncharitably. Not that I'd anything to hide.

"Viva Las Vegas! Have a good time, kiddo," she said as she waved me off. Kiddo. She'd picked that up from Roger, I bet. No one else I knew ever used that expression.

IT WAS REMARKABLE how little had changed since the last time I had driven across the Mojave to Las Vegas. Even the desert tortoise I swerved to avoid might well have been the same one, still making his laborious and hazardous way across the interstate.

Apart from Roger's death, my life hadn't changed much either. I was still driving the Ford Country Squire, which, now two years older, had not improved with age. But then, who had? But it served me well enough for my pet detecting business, being impervious to dings and roomy enough for the traps, cages, catch-poles, and other paraphernalia required to ply my trade.

It did, however, leave something to be desired on a trip across the desert where the summer temperature could soar to one hundred and fifteen degrees; air-conditioning being the most notable lack. I alternated between having the windows open, when the hot desert air blew in my face like an overheated hair dryer, and having the windows closed, which proved unbearable. Even my cotton shorts and tank top felt like too much clothing.

"If we strike it rich in Las Vegas, we'll buy a new car, one with air-conditioning, Watson old girl." Her nose out the window, Watson was not really paying much attention to anything I might have to say. She'd heard it all before, and no doubt knew as well as I that I was never going to be able to afford a new car on what I earned as a pet detective.

I had Lulu, the Pekingese, to thank for my new career. Word of my success in finding her had quickly spread through our small seaside town, and, after the *Surf City News* ran the story, people began calling on me for assistance in locating their own lost pets. At first I had tried to help on an informal basis, but eventually, as the advertising and travel expenses mounted, I started to charge a fee. I had business cards made up, sent out flyers to all the shelters in the southwest region, and declared myself a Pet P.I.

Tracing lost dogs and cats is not as easy as it sounds. You have to think quickly and move fast. As I had learned very early on with Lulu, a lost pet can travel miles before it's found. If it gets to an animal shelter, it has a better chance of being located, but people are often reluctant to turn a pet in, and that can mean it might never get back to its owner. Then again, if a pet isn't claimed from a shelter within the specified holding period, usually a week, it may be put to sleep. If it's adopted, the new owner is under no obligation to return the pet to its original owner should he or she eventually show up.

"It's not the least bit elementary, is it, my dear Watson?" I said as she restlessly moved around on the backseat trying to find a cool spot.

"Better not get into that," I warned as she sniffed at an unfamiliar cardboard box. But there was no real danger. I'd taped it very securely. It contained the illegal steel-jaw trap that I'd intended to drop off at Fish & Game. Recent events had put it clean out of my head.

Once I'd made up my mind to turn pro, I decided that the time had come for me to get the dog companion I had always longed for. My experience with Lulu had exposed me to life's seamier side, and I decided that a large protective dog would suit me best.

That's when Watson came into my life. She had been a washout at her first two careers: motherhood and guard dog. In the latter case, she just hadn't been able to grasp what was expected of a dog with her breed's reputation. But she was exactly what I was looking for. Five years old, with a gentle temperament, but an appearance that would hopefully keep us both out of trouble. A sheep in wolf's clothing, if ever I saw one. I'd found her at the shelter. Or she'd found me. I'd walked past her cage, felt those liquid brown eyes following me, turned back, and it was love at first sight. I think we have both benefitted from the partnership.

"Never mind, luv, we'll soon be there," I said as she jumped from the back to the front seat, trying to get comfortable.

"Where will you be staying?" both Posey and Mallory had asked.

"I'll let you know when I get there," I'd replied. The truth was, I hadn't a clue. But there was little else in Las Vegas but hotels and motels, and I didn't expect to have any trouble finding accommodation. But though I saw plenty of flashing-neon vacancy signs as I made my way through the town, not one of them indicated that pets were welcome. It had completely slipped my mind, the difficulty I'd had finding a place to take Lulu the last time I was in Las Vegas. I had ended up staying at the Twilight Zone Motel that time. I certainly had no intention of going back there again.

I was almost out of town when I spotted a pets welcome sign. It was at the entrance to an RV campground offering 350 full utility spaces, hookups, twenty-four hour convenience store, pool, and, wonder of wonders, a fenced pet run.

"This looks like the place for us, Watson, old girl," I said, turning into the driveway of the Lucky Hitch. "Let's trust that the fact that we don't have a trailer doesn't exclude us."

My trust was misplaced. This time it was not my dog but myself who was persona non grata.

I was greeted in the office by a pigeon-shaped little woman, top-heavy in the bosom, whose name tag announced her to be Glenda Grackle, manager. In her sixties, I would guess, she wore a bright red and white floral caftan, the rollers in her hair covered with a pink net.

The rollers shook with disapproval when in answer to her inquiry as to what size space I needed, I explained that I had hoped she would have units to rent. Otherwise, perhaps I could purchase a tent?

"Can't do that," she said, going on to explain that the facility was exclusively for the use of guests with fully equipped motor homes of their own. "And definitely no tents," she finished with a sniff.

I looked around at the sleek motor homes dotting the premises, air conditioners and television antennas sprouting from every roof. Camping had entered a whole new era since I had slept under canvas with the Brownies back home in Mossy Wood.

I was sitting in the car outside the campground office, pondering my next move, when Watson's low growl and a tap on the window got my attention.

A familiar voice demanded, "Delilah! Is that you?"

9

Old Friends

I LOOKED UP in astonishment. Peering in the window, large as life and twice as friendly, were Alf and Gert Pickles, the couple from Blackpool in England's north country, whom I'd met when I'd located their lost Basset hound, Bertie, some months back. He'd wandered off while they were vacationing in Southern California, and each had thought the other had put him in the car. The last I heard they were living in Elko, Nevada. I had never expected to ever set eyes on them again.

They might have been siblings they looked so much alike. Their fair round faces, touched with the high colour born of England's brisk winters, beamed good naturedly down at me. Curly-haired, his grey, hers faded blond, both wearing denim shorts, red tank tops, and blue flip-flops.

I rolled down the window. "Well, this is a surprise!"

Gert was the first to speak. "I'll say. I says to 'is nibs, I says, ' 'Ere, that don't 'alf look like Delilah's old car.' We never could understand why you drove such an old banger, you being so ladylike an' all. And 'is nibs says, ' 'Ee by gum, luv, you're right. And that's Watson along with 'er.' "

I got out of the car and was soon engulfed in the

embraces of the two large and friendly people.

"And 'ere's our Bertie," said Gert, indicating the grey-snouted Basset at their feet. "Say 'allo to Delilah, Bertie. She's the one what saved you from the fertilizer factory."

Bertie gazed at me with huge, doleful eyes, then glanced uncertainly at Watson, who was wagging her tail in tentative greeting. After the requisite initial sniffings, they each decided the other could be tolerated.

Leaning down to pet the elderhound, I asked "What are you doing here?"

"We've been in town for a couple of days to see our attorney," they said.

I was embarrassed they would think I was prying into their affairs. "Actually, what I meant was, what are you doing *here,* in this campground."

They explained that they had just recently bought their motor home. "After losing our Bertie like that, we thought we'd be better off if we could take him with us wherever we went," said Gert. "So much nicer for the poor little love. He don't like being left. We had such a scare that time you found him for us, we don't want to go through that again. We reckon that with the motor home, we'll have somewhere familiar he can stay, all comfy like, if we have to leave him for a short while."

"Come and have a shufty," said Alf.

With Watson alongside, I followed them across the dusty, eucalyptus-shaded campground, my friends explaining as we went that they had moved from Elko to the Overton area, northeast of Las Vegas, a few months back.

"Let's 'ave a cup of tea," said Gert as soon as we

stepped inside to the welcome cool blast from the two air conditioner units. "I'll put the kettle on while you have a look around." The Pickles' combined girth seemed to fill the entire coach, and it rocked gently every time one of them moved.

Business must be good, I thought. Theirs was the largest coach in the campground; it needed to be to accommodate people of their build. The oversized, custom-made fittings provided every comfort and convenience necessary to travel in style. From the television, microwave oven, and refrigerator, to the kingsize bed and the bathroom with a sunken tub, all was luxury. Yet it still had the feel of home. The walls were hung with photos of Bertie and people whom I took to be friends or family members, a cross-stitched sampler bearing the Union Jack and the legend "God Save the Queen," and a map of southern Nevada.

Gert poured tea from a pot as big as a bucket. "Now tell us what brings you here," she said.

I gave them the short version, saying only that I was in Las Vegas on business and hadn't had any luck finding a place that would accept pets. When I said it looked like I'd be sleeping in my car, they were horrified.

"Oh, you don't want to do that, luv," said Alf. "That's not safe. We've got plenty of room." He patted the upholstered bench we were sitting on. "This 'ere makes into a bed." He turned to his wife. "She can muck in with us, can't she, luv?"

"Of course, she can. Can't do enough for Delilah, not since you saved our Bertie," agreed Gert, gazing fondly at the Basset who, having decided that Watson offered no threat, had curled up alongside her at my feet.

The offer was genuine, but I wasn't sure that, spacious as it was, there was room for a third party in the motor home.

That evening we ate at a picnic table under the stars. The air was filled with the sound of crickets and, from the brightly lit swimming pool, came the excited laughter of children, every so often with the slap of the convenience store screen door. The store stocked everything from Calor gas to frozen steaks, along with a couple of slot machines for those who couldn't be bothered to drive a half-mile to the nearest casino to lose their money.

Glenda Grackle, a laundry basket under one arm, a small child under the other, made her way to the Laundromat. It seemed like another world. Hard to realize the glitz and glamour of Las Vegas was so close by.

Despite the heat, Gert had insisted on cooking a big English dinner in my honor, and though I couldn't do the steak and kidney pudding, mashed potatoes and gravy, and brussels sprouts the justice I would have on a cold winter night, it was nevertheless welcome. It was months since I'd enjoyed true English cooking. In Southern California, both the climate and the health-conscious culture encouraged lighter meals.

Under the picnic table, Watson and Bertie were getting better acquainted over bowls of kibble generously garnished with steak and kidney pudding leftovers. Watson was in heaven. No such table scraps came her way at home. Nor mine, for that matter.

My hosts elaborated on the reasons for their visit to Las Vegas.

"Nothing serious, I hope," I said.

"Well it's complicated, like, but it has to do with our ostriches," said Alf.

"Ostriches?"

"Didn't we tell you? That's what we're raising on our new ranch. Ostriches. Doing very nicely, thank you very much, what with the sidelines an' all, and the chicks bringing three thousand apiece." I almost choked on my tea. I was definitely in the wrong business. "But just recently Big Gus, our best male, has been right poorly, and when we called the vet—"

Gert started to laugh and wiped her eyes as the tears rolled down her face. Her whole body was shaking. Alf just shook his head and grinned.

"Oh, what a to-do that was," she finally got out between chuckles. " 'Ee fair got the 'ump when we told 'im it was the ostriches. 'Hostriches,' says 'e, all hoity-toity like. 'I'm a farm vet, not a zoo vet.' Tell 'er, Alf."

Alf took up the story. " 'Well,' says I, 'this 'ere's a farm ostrich. Sommat's making 'im sick, and I'd like to know what the 'ell it is.' "

"Well, old Big Gus, he don't like being messed about with at the best of times, and when he's feeling poorly, or in mating season, he can turn cantankerous and down-right ugly. 'E chased that vet round and round the paddock—forty miles an hour them birds can run—'til finally the poor man jumped clean over the five foot chainlink fence."

By this time both of them were helpless with laughter and neither could speak.

"Then what happened?" I prompted, laughing with them.

" 'E 'ad to get his tranquilizer gun to calm Big Gus

down," said Gert, wiping her eyes with the corner of her apron.

"So that's why you're here to see your attorney, because the vet harmed your ostrich?"

"Oh no, lord luv yer. He did his job right and proper. 'E's a lovely man, is our vet. And 'andsome. A right bobby-dazzler."

"Aye," put in Alf, with markedly less enthusiasm. " 'Andsome is as 'andsome does."

"Oh, give over. You're just jealous," said Gert, digging him in the ribs. "Any road up, 'e checked Big Gus over well and good once he couldn't put up an argument. Took a blood test and blow me down if he didn't find that Big Gus had some kind of poisoning. He thought it might be something in the soil and suggested we might have to consider moving."

"Funny," said Alf. "It's happened three times. The vet gets him better, but the day after he leaves, blowed if old Gus don't get poorly again."

They had consulted their attorney to see if they had a case against the party who sold them the land for not disclosing that it was unsafe for animals, at least not safe for ostriches.

"What did he say?"

"He doesn't think so, but he's going to make inquiries and get back to us," said Alf.

Knowing nothing about ostriches, and still less about toxic soil, I wasn't able to offer much help. But all they really needed was an appreciative audience for their story.

A jollier couple you couldn't hope to meet. They laughed at each other's jokes, and as long as I joined in the laughter, they didn't seem to expect much else from me. They delighted in each other's company and appeared to be as much in love as the day they'd married. As I warmed to them, it crossed my mind that compared to theirs, my life seemed empty indeed.

"Ee by gum, she's a caution that one. Don't know how I'd get along without her," said Alf, after Gert, rocking with laughter, had gone back into the coach to put the kettle on for another cup of tea. "How come you've never married, lass?"

This was a question so fraught with the unexplainable, that I hesitated before answering. Finally I said, "I was married once, but he died." I turned away to watch Glenda returning with her laundry basket, the child now asleep on top of the clean clothes. "I'd rather not talk about it if you don't mind."

"Sorry, lass. Didn't mean to pry. Just so as you know that if ever you need a hand, me and Gert would be only too happy to oblige."

It was getting late and what I mostly needed was a place to stay. The Pickles repeated their offer to let me bunk in with them. I knew it would be a squeeze, and with two large dogs thrown in for good measure. However, I didn't see that I had much choice. The campground had been my last resort.

"Well, just for tonight then," I said gratefully, since they would brook no argument. "Tomorrow, when I'm fresh, I'll see about finding another place."

"Tell you what," said Alf. "We're off 'ome tomorrow afternoon. We 'ave to get back to check on Big Gus. 'E's on a special diet now. But you can stay here, and we'll take your car. You can drive the coach back to our place when you've done with your business."

"Oh, I couldn't let you do that," I protested, horrified at the thought of taking the big rig on the road. "My car doesn't have air-conditioning."

"It's only about sixty miles," he persisted. "My lord, lass, it's the least we can do for you after you saved our Bertie's life. That way you'll have to come and visit us, just like we always wanted you to."

I felt like I'd been burdened with the curse that holds that once you've saved somebody's life, you were stuck with them forever. Sweet as they were, visiting the Pickles' ostrich ranch was not high on my list of fantasy vacations, and I gently, but firmly, told them there was no way I would push them out of their motor home. I wasn't sure I'd trust myself to drive it, anyway.

Before going to bed I took Watson for a walk, stopping by the pay phone outside the store to call home and retrieve my messages in case any urgent assignments had come in since I'd left. I was surprised to find that the line was busy.

"Drat that Poscy," I said to Watson. "Why is she there so late? I hope she's not making long-distance calls at our expense."

. 10 .

Taking Care of Business

THE NEXT MORNING I awoke to the delicious smell of a real English breakfast: bacon, eggs, grilled mushrooms, tomatoes, and fried bread.

I quickly straightened up the bedclothes and folded the cot back into its bench seat position.

"Here you go, Delilah," said Gert, setting a plate in front of me at the dinette. I realized why we had dined al fresco the previous evening. There was no way Gert and Alf could have squeezed into the tiny dining area.

"It looks scrumptious, but, really, I couldn't touch a bite," I said, pushing the plate away. It was not appetite, but memories of meals at home that had set my mouth salivating. "Tea is all I can face, first thing in the morning."

"Lor' luv-a-duck," exclaimed my hostess. "No wonder you're such a slip of a thing. You need to get outside a good breakfast of a morning to keep your strength up."

We compromised on toast and marmalade, which I really did enjoy. I had forgotten how good Keiller's Dundee marmalade tasted. As soon as I got back to Surf City I would have to make a special trip to get some from the British Grocer, where all the local ex-pats got their nostalgia food fix.

"You're teaching me bad habits." I laughed when Gert set a second plate of hot buttered toast in front of me.

From behind the bedroom partition came the sound of snoring. Alf was still asleep.

" 'E needs 'is beauty rest," chuckled his wife. "Just as well 'e sleeps late. I can't stand 'aving 'im underfoot when I'm trying to fix meals in this doll's house."

I bathed in the sunken tub. It was bigger than the bath in my house, and I would have liked to have soaked longer in Gert's lavender bath salts, but I had business to attend to. This was the day I might find out if I was heiress to a silver mine.

Alf and Gert had given me the name of their attorney. They didn't know him well, they said. He was someone their vet had referred them to. But he had seemed "a decent enough chappie."

I pulled on a pair of tan shorts and a green T-shirt, slipped my feet into white tennies, and slathered face and arms with sun block. Not expecting my business to take more than a day or so, I had brought only one change of shorts and a T-shirt, plus a sweater and jeans in case the weather should turn chilly. Not much chance of that. A blast of hot air hit me as soon as I stepped outside the motor home, though it was only 9 A.M.

With Watson in tow, I made my way to the Laundromat to wash the shorts and T-shirt I had worn the previous day.

"Don't give her any quarters," Gert called after me. I soon learned what she meant.

Glenda Grackle, her hair still in rollers, was unloading bed linen from a dryer. I was about to remark that her laundry chores seemed endless, when she volunteered the information that she did it for campground guests for a small charge.

"Next time you need laundry done, just drop it off at the store," she said. She folded the last of the sheets, then said, "Do you have any change? I've run out."

I fished in my pocket and handed her a couple of quarters, which she promptly fed into the slot machine sharing wall space with the soap dispenser. It failed to produce the desired jackpot, and I wondered if she would have shared her winnings with me if it had proved otherwise.

"One of these days . . ." Glenda shrugged resignedly. "Thanks. I'll take it off your tab at the store." I refrained from commenting that I wasn't running a tab. But I could see what her game was. Doing the laundry to the exclusion of almost everybody else in the campground gave her a much better chance of winning when the machine eventually paid off.

I set my laundry going, then took Watson for a walk around the park. We stopped by the fenced pet playground where a couple of Beagles, with much yapping, chased a soccer ball. They were unsupervised, unless it was by the small boy leaning against the fence engrossed in a handheld video game. I opened the gate and turned Watson loose to join in the fun. The Beagles backed away from the ball when they saw the big Dobie bearing down on them, but once they realized she was not going to bully them, they set the ball rolling again, with Watson bounding forward like a little goalie whenever it came in her direction.

It was too hot to keep the game going for long, and

as soon as Watson sat down in the shade of the fence I knew she'd had enough.

I waved to a family eating breakfast under an awning extending from the roof of their motor home. Everyone seemed very relaxed, quite different from the frantic pace I had observed along the Strip the previous evening. If you could gamble while you did your wash, why go any farther to throw money away?

Before picking up my laundry, I stopped at the pay phone again to check my messages. This time the line was free.

The first message concerned a raccoon. My classified ads attracted a fair number of calls having nothing whatever to do with lost and found pets. It was as if by advertising expertise in one area of animal welfare I was, by implication, claiming to be an expert in all others.

"I need help with a raccoon," a woman's voice said. "I don't want it harmed, but it's a nuisance. It's coming in through the cat door and eating my kitty's food. I'm sure it was the raccoon because he ate the peanut butter cups, too."

"How does she know that kitty didn't steal the candy?" I said to Watson, who waited patiently by my side. I would call the woman back as soon as I got home and advise her to nail the cat flap shut and solve two problems at once: keep wildlife out and the cat in. "If there are raccoons around, there are probably coyotes, too," I said to Watson. "Kitty will use up her nine lives in a hurry if she continues to go outside."

Watson tried to look sympathetic, but she'd heard it all before. Some people just didn't get it. They move to an area because of its pleasant environment, then set about destroying the very qualities that had made it attractive to them in the first place. They seemed quite unable to accept that they are the intruders and that they should learn to co-exist with the wildlife.

The second call was from Evie. "Delilah, are you there? Do pick up, there's a sweetie." Her cut-glass English tones sounded out of place in this most American of American places. "Howard's just got back from Texas, where he came across some rather interesting information about Roger. A friend of a friend says that they'd heard he'd somehow got hold of some property in Nevada. It's quite outrageous that he didn't tell you about it. But then, what did we expect? Anyway, the important thing is that there might be a tiny bit of money coming your way. I can't wait to see you. I'll be there on your doorstep tomorrow afternoon to tell all."

A tiny bit of money coming my way. Well that was nice, especially as Evie's tiny bit would very likely be anybody else's large amount. And could it be the same piece of property I had recently discovered the deed to? I looked at my watch. It was too late to call her back and tell her I was out of town. She was probably already on her way to Surf City. Never mind. Posey would tell her where I was.

Evie would naturally be excited to think she might have uncovered something to my advantage. I knew she felt partially responsible for my disastrous marriage to Roger. A new bride herself, she had, quite understandably, been very taken up with Howard at the time. Nevertheless, she felt she hadn't done enough to dissuade me from making what turned out to be a huge mistake, and ever since Roger's death she had made it her personal quest to marry me off to one of her Really Nice Men. Trouble was, her idea of nice and mine didn't always coincide. Wealth and looks were Evie's primary concern, while mine, particularly after the hard lessons learned from marriage to Roger, ran more along the lines of compatability and honesty.

Next I put in a call to Posey. Since she didn't have pets of her own I wasn't sure she'd be able to cope with mine. I left a message on her machine letting her know where I was and that I hoped everything was okay. Love to Hobo and Dolly.

Thanks to gambling Glenda I had barely enough change left by the time I got around to calling the attorney.

When I explained to the young woman who answered the telephone that I was only in town for a couple of days, she obliged by fitting me in that very morning. So, leaving Watson with Alf and Gert, I headed downtown to the attorney's office.

Mort Falco, middle-aged and thickset, positively gleamed well-being from the top of his shiny bald head, past his expensive shiny silk suit, to the tips of his manicured fingers.

He stood up when I entered his office and indicated I take a seat in the chair opposite him.

The preliminaries taken care of, I told him that I had recently come across an interesting document that indicated I might be the owner of some Nevada real estate.

He made notes on a yellow pad, then took the deed from me and looked it over. For the first time since I had entered his office he seemed to show real interest in my case.

He leaned forward across the desk, his chin thrust out, eyes narrowing beneath bushy silver brows. "Who did you say referred you?"

"Mr. Alf Pickles. He was here to see you yesterday."

"Have you discussed this business with him?"

"No. I thought it best to say nothing to anyone until I was sure of what it all meant."

"Very wise," he nodded. "And I advise you to continue to say nothing until we're sure of the facts."

He studied the document further, then said, "You realize that the paper is torn just here?" He indicated with the tip of his pencil. "The parcel number is incomplete."

I nodded. "Yes, I noticed that."

"I'll have to call Carson City and make inquiries. It will take a little while to trace. Check back with me tomorrow morning."

I was unable to hide my disappointment that I wouldn't know anything for at least another twenty-four hours. But there was nothing for it. I would have to tell Gert and Alf that my business would keep me in Vegas another day. If they were still willing, I would like to take them up on their offer to let me stay in the motor home and drive it out to their ranch the following day, come what may. There shouldn't be too many cars on the country roads, and I would drive really slowly and carefully.

"Of course, luv. That'll be perfect. Just what we wanted all along," said Alf in his kindly way. "We'd stay here with you, but like I said before, we've got to get back to take care of Big Gus."

"It's an easy drive," he said, pointing out the route on

the map on the wall. "Shouldn't take you more than two hours, tops. There's the keys." He indicated a bunch of keys hanging on a hook just inside the coach door.

Before they left I retrieved Watson's kibble from the back of the station wagon. I was about to close the tailgate when I caught sight of the box containing the trap. I didn't really think Gert or Alf would pry, but if they did the consequences could be disastrous. To be on the safe side I took the box with me into the coach.

And then, amid more hugs, Gert, Alf and Bertie left the campground in my old crate, leaving Watson and me to rattle around in their luxury motor home all by ourselves.

I fell asleep that night thinking about my visit to the lawyer, excited about what the morning might bring, and wondering why it should take him so long to research what, after all, seemed to be quite a simple matter. He was, of course, charging by the hour.

I reached out and stroked Watson's head. "Well, if he has good news for us, who cares about the bill?"

. 11 .

Misgivings

I AWOKE FULL of foreboding. Not at all so sure I was up to taking this giant rig out onto an unfamiliar road, especially after a closer look at the wall map indicated some nasty looking zigzags, which could only be mountain bends.

It took several cups of tea, and some more marmalade and toast, to restore my optimism. How hard could it be? It was only about sixty miles.

I made an inspection of the business end of the coach. Two extremely comfortable captain's chairs for driver and copilot, a dashboard that looked like the console of a DC-10. Huge side mirrors. Automatic transmission. It was probably easier to handle than my ancient wagon.

Alf had informed Glenda Grackle that I had permission to take the coach, and the rent had been paid until the end of the week, including something extra for her husband, George, who was to assist me in disengaging the electricity, water, and tank hookups.

I tidied up and made a quick survey to ensure everything was safely stowed away, as Gert had requested, then walked over to the store to let them know I was ready to leave. George was nowhere in sight.

"He'll be there in a few minutes. He's fixing one of

the dryers," said the perpetually rollered Glenda. Did she ever remove those things? Her hair must be peculiarly resistant to waves. Was there some big occasion coming up that she was saving her curls for?

I decided to make a couple of calls while I waited. It was too early to call the attorney, so I dialled home to check if anything more profitable than peanut-butter eating raccoons needed my attention. Or perhaps Evie had tried to reach me again.

A man answered the telephone. "Who's this?" The voice was official and abrupt.

"I'm sorry. I must have dialled the wrong number," I said.

"Delilah?"

It was Jack Mallory.

"I say. What are you doing in my house?" I blurted out.

"Where are you?" he countered.

"You know where I am. In Las Vegas. You've got a check being in my house when—"

"Delilah, listen," he broke in, his voice tight with concern. "There's a problem here. Someone's been killed in your house. It's your neighbour, Posey Brightman."

"Posey? Killed? In my house?" I repeated the words, but none of them made any sense.

"Listen," he said again, urgently. "You've got to be careful. It's possible that whoever did this thought it was you. What was she doing here?"

I became aware Glenda was hovering nearby, having taken a sudden interest in cleaning the store window. I turned away from her and lowered my voice.

"She's looking after Dolly and Hobo while I'm gone."

I wasn't yet used to the idea that Posey was dead and continued to speak of her in the present tense.

There was a pause while he digested this information. Probably trying to figure out who Hobo and Dolly were. "Where's your car?"

"My car?"

"Don't keep repeating everything I say. Where's your car?"

"Why?"

"The killer, or killers, there may be more than one, probably know what you're driving. Once they realize their mistake they'll be on the lookout for it. Get rid of it. Park it somewhere and get a rental."

"That's no problem. I'm not driving it . . ." My voice trailed off as I realized that Alf and Gert had taken my car.

I struggled to control my voice. "How did you find her?"

"Your friend Mrs. Cavendish was looking for you. When she couldn't get in, she looked in the window and saw the body. She called us. She's very upset. Naturally, she thought it was you. So did I." I could hear the pain in his voice and realized what a horrible shock this had been for my friends.

"Oh, no. Where is she?"

"She's with your other neighbour across the street, Ariel Ferris. Wait. The coroner's just arrived." He put the phone down for a minute. I could hear him talking to someone.

He came back on the phone. "Delilah, I've got to go. You have to understand that you're in danger. Where are you right now?"

"I'm at the Lucky Hitch. It's an RV campground on the outskirts of town."

"A campground!" I could hear the exasperation in his voice. Hardly the most secure location with a killer on the loose.

"I'm fine. No one knows I'm here except the Pickles."

"The Pickles?"

Now who was repeating? "Friends of mine. Don't worry. I've known them forever. Besides, they're English."

"That's no guarantee of anything," he said gruffly. "I want you to sit tight. I'm going to call Las Vegas PD and have them send someone over to keep an eye on you."

"I don't need a baby-sitter. Watson's here, and the campground is very secure." I thought of Glenda in her rollers, her husband in the Laundromat. Some security. "Anyway, if they think I'm already dead, why do I need to be scared?"

"Don't argue, Delilah." He hung up before I had a chance to ask him if he'd mind checking on Dolly's and Hobo's food dishes. Never mind. It would have seemed a little insensitive with Posey lying dead in my house. Apparently Ariel was back. I'd call and ask her to take care of them.

Mallory would do what he saw fit. But I had no intention of staying at the campground to see who got here first, the police or those who for some reason or another wanted to do me in.

Questions and recriminations bounced around in my head. Had Posey been mistaken for me? Was it my fault she was dead? Why hadn't I listened to Mallory and

Tony when they advised me against the trip? Why hadn't I just stayed home and consulted a Surf City attorney? Of course, in that case, I might well be the one lying dead in my house right now.

The answers were all too obvious. I was in this predicament because I was stubborn and didn't like people telling me what to do.

I was dismayed to realize that Alf and Gert were in danger because of me. I had to warn them. If Mallory was right and my car was indeed a target, then they were in more jeopardy than I. If any harm should come to them it would be my fault. Of course, they would be home by now, but who knew at what point the killer had realized his mistake. I didn't know how long Posey had been dead. Had the killer had time to get to Las Vegas by plane? Or might he have alerted an accomplice to track down my car?

Where once I had been a reluctant visitor to the ostrich ranch, now I couldn't get there fast enough. If I'd had their number I would have telephoned the Pickles to warn them. But I didn't have their number, and it would take too long to find it, precious time when I could be on the road. And what if there was really no cause for alarm? I didn't want to scare them unnecessarily. It was only sixty miles. I could be there in not much more than an hour.

While I was on the telephone, George Grackle had emerged from the Laundromat and was making his way to the motor home to detach it from its life-support systems.

"Ever driven one of these babies before?" he asked.

"Oh yes," I lied, afraid that if I said no he'd feel

obliged to give me all kinds of lessons and delay my departure.

"Good. They can be a bit tricky on the mountain roads. Take it nice and easy, and you'll be fine." he said.

There was no turning back now. "Here goes, Watson," I said to my sidekick, already settled in the co-pilot's seat as if to the manor born. I turned the key, put the thing into drive, and headed for the fortunately wide exit. "We'll be okay as long as we don't have to back up."

As we exited the campground, from the corner of my eye I saw a Las Vegas PD patrol car enter at the other end of the park. "Too bad, lads, you just missed us," I said under my breath.

Driving a truck was probably like this. I wouldn't know. The coach was so wide it was almost impossible to see what was behind us. Now I knew why the big side mirrors were necessary. But after a few near misses and false starts, inviting indignantly honked horns at traffic signals, I began to feel more confident. For the first part of the journey we travelled on I-15, a continuation of the highway we'd come in on from California—long, straight, and uninteresting. Ideal for a novice. The best thing, of course, was the air-conditioning.

"Piece of cake, Watson, old girl," I said. "Maybe we'll get one of these for ourselves once we sell the property."

We hit a pothole and Watson looked dubious, obviously not quite as confident of my ability to handle this house on wheels as I was.

We were well out of town by the time I remembered I hadn't called the attorney back. That would have to wait. Reaching Alf and Gert before anything dire happened to them was the priority now.

The encounter with the pothole was bothering me, and, after we'd turned off the interstate, I decided I'd better check to see if there was any damage before tackling the mountain drive. "More haste, less speed," I said to Watson as I pulled into a rest stop offering easy in and out access. I parked in the shade of a large billboard that shielded us from the sight of the road.

The motor home refrigerator worked on batteries when not hooked up and was generously stocked with cool drinks, half an apple pie, and some sausage rolls. "Good. Some munchies to eat on our way," I told my sidekick.

We stepped outside to stretch our legs. I was watching the road while waiting for Watson to finish taking care of her personal business when a Corvette went by at a high rate of speed. Not just any Corvette, but a bilious green job with an orange flame painted on the side. Surely there couldn't be two such monstrosities? I was still watching it hurtle down the dusty road when I heard another vehicle approaching. It was driving fast, though it couldn't match the Corvette's speed.

There was no doubt at all as to whom this one belonged.

. 12 .

Hue and Cry

THERE COULD BE no mistaking Tony's woody, his surf-board attached to the roof-rack. But it was impossible to tell if he was trying to catch up with the Corvette or merely following it. What in the world was he up to? Clearly his presence on a remote Nevada highway indicated he knew far more about my business than he had let on when he had asked me to take care of Trixie back in Surf City. Had he intended to come here all along? Or had he changed his mind once he knew I was headed this way?

Had both cars been following me? And who was driving what I had once thought to be Roger's Corvette? It was too much of a coincidence to think that Tony, the Corvette's driver, and myself, all just happened to be on the same road at the same time. From what Mallory had told me, it was quite possible that the Corvette's driver, at least, was on the trail of the Country Squire, which he would assume I was driving. Was Tony attempting to head them off? Or was he in league with them?

At that point I would have much preferred to turn around and go in search of the nearest friendly police-man. But the only ones likely to take me seriously were back in Las Vegas, and I was way out of their jurisdic-

tion by then. And what crime could I report? None! In
any case, there was no time. Alf and Gert could be in
danger. I had to warn them. Besides, there appeared to
be only one way to get to the bottom of this mystery.
Keep heading toward the ostrich farm.

Neither the Pickles nor myself had made any secret
of where I was going. It didn't even occur to me until I
spoke to Mallory that it might be a problem. Anyone
trailing me to the Lucky Hitch could have found out
where I'd gone after I left there. If Glenda had shown
the slightest reluctance to be forthcoming with the information, I'm sure she could be bought for a handful
of quarters. Would she have told the police also? She
must have had a field day after I left. First the Corvette
driver, then Tony, and finally the police, all anteing up
quarters.

Of course, once they knew I'd left the city, the Las
Vegas police would consider their obligation discharged.
I wasn't wanted for anything. They had been doing a
colleague a favour by checking up on me. There wasn't
the slightest chance they would give chase.

But how had my pursuers traced me to the campground? I had told no one except Mallory, who had,
presumably, informed the police. Who else knew?
Glenda and George Grackle. And I'd left a message for
Posey. Then there was the attorney, of course, and his
secretary. When he asked for my telephone number, I'd
told him I was staying at the Lucky Hitch RV park and
would have to use a public phone, so I would call him.
It began to look like the shorter list would be who *hadn't*
I told.

Munchies and pothole dings forgotten, I hustled Wat-

son back into the coach and pulled out onto the highway.
There was no way I could catch up with the Corvette,
but maybe, with luck, I could overtake Tony, flag him
down and insist he give me an explanation. I had always
known that his past did not bear much scrutiny. He was
a self-confessed petty thief, and had had more than one
brush with the law. But he'd assured me on so many
occasions that he had retired and that those days were
behind him, I had come to believe him.

As we covered the miles, the fears mounted. Here I
was, driving a borrowed luxury motor home in the middle of the Nevada desert at, while not breakneck, definitely unsafe speed, pursuing a man I had thought to be
my friend but now, for all I knew, might turn out to be
involved in the death of my husband. There was a dead
woman lying in my house who had, in all probability,
been mistaken for me. My home had been broken into—
not once but twice—and my best friend had suffered a
terrible shock.

And someone driving a sports car in the poorest possible taste was chasing two dear, innocent people because they had been so kind as to trade vehicles with
me.

We were now in the mountains, and the road switched
back and forth. One moment I felt crushed against the
side of the mountain as I pulled close in to avoid on-
coming traffic, the next I was terrified the heavy rig was
going to drag us over the edge into the canyon below.
Desperate though I was to reach the ranch, I dared not
go any faster. I glanced anxiously at Watson. She was
on her feet, sliding from side to side in the big captain's
chair. I wished she'd sit down. But she was too nervous.

Belatedly I realized I should have attempted to fasten the seatbelt around her before we'd started out.

I heaved a sigh of relief when at last we headed down the mountain and neared the turnoff Alf had told me to watch for. I slowed down to get my bearings. I was running low on petrol and pulled into a gas station at the crossroads. There was no attendant. It was one of those robot places where you put in your credit card and pump the petrol yourself. I didn't like these things at the best of times, and this was not one of the best. I wasted precious minutes first manoeuvering the coach into the station, then getting out to figure out where to put in the petrol. Of course, I'd pulled in on the wrong side. Being extremely reluctant to attempt backing up, I had to drive out onto the road, and do a U-turn to get back in on the correct side. All this used up precious time. If there'd been an attendant at least I could have told him to hurry up, and maybe he could have told me if a Corvette or an old woody station wagon had passed that way.

Back on the highway, I was surprised to find a marked change in the landscape. Gone were the desert vistas. We were entering a fertile valley with trees, crops, and herds of cattle.

There was still no sign of Tony or the Corvette. Alf had told me that there were two routes I could take, the scenic and the direct. I must have inadvertently taken the scenic, and it now occurred to me that Tony and the green monster might have gone the direct route and had already reached the ostrich ranch.

At last I came to the sign I'd been watching for. Instead of the usual "Lazy L," or "Crooked K" type sign customary on western ranches, the one over the entrance to the Pickles' spread gave a very typically English "Dun Roamin'." Another sign, tacked to the fence, must have originally read "Pickles Ostrich Farm," but some wag had changed the *s* in Pickles to a *d*. A thought to boggle the mind as I made my way along the dusty road leading to the ranch house and outbuildings.

The Country Squire was parked in the driveway, but there was no sign of either the Corvette or the Woody. For a moment my hopes rose, thinking that maybe I had jumped to all the wrong conclusions and that whatever Tony and the Corvette driver were up to, it had nothing to do with me.

Such hopes were dashed as soon as I had parked the coach alongside my station wagon. I felt physically sick. My car had been thoroughly turned over. The upholstery ripped, the seats pulled out of place. The rear door was down. It was with some surprise that I saw the keys were still in the ignition.

Except for the occasional rooster crow and the hum of distant farm machinery, it was strangely quiet. Too quiet for a ranch that must normally have been bustling with activity. I reached into the back of the wagon and grabbed the catch-pole, a long stick with a noose on the end I used on rare occasions to snare a fearful runaway pet. It was hardly a weapon, but it was better than nothing.

I approached the house afraid of what I might find. The front door stood open, and after calling out "Alf? Gert?" a couple of times, with no real expectation of a reply, I entered, holding Watson by the collar, close to my side.

A strange whistling sound was coming from the rear

of the house. I followed it to the kitchen and found a large red, enamel teakettle on a high, gas flame, whistling itself dry. I reached over and turned off the gas. They had made it indoors then. I experienced a sense of dread as I imagined the intruders bursting in on my friends just as they settled down for a nice cuppa after their journey.

Catch-pole in hand, and Watson close beside me, I returned to the yard to check the outbuildings, disturbing a flock of chickens listless in the afternoon heat. Across the yard I could see the ostrich paddock that Gert had so laughingly described in her vet story, and the cornstalk-tall (eight or nine feet, I would guess) scrubby heads of a couple of ostriches. One of them must be Big Gus. I would have liked to have taken a closer look, but I could not spare the time. Catching wind of the ostriches, Watson stiffened, sniffed the air, and prepared to bark. "Shh," I said, before she could utter a woof.

With mounting fear for my friends' well-being, I checked the nearest barn, stifling a sneeze. The heat heightened the smell of the bales of alfalfa stacked neatly to one side. I had heard that ostriches would eat anything. It was surprising that, according to the vet, something in the soil here was upsetting so sturdy a character as the three hundred pound Gus.

A sudden noise startled me, and I leaped back, almost falling over Watson, close behind. But it was only a bird in the rafters. Probably a barn owl. Still, it seemed to me there was another creature there. I thought I could hear breathing, shuffling in the gloom.

"Who's there?" I called. "Alf? Gert?" No response. Gradually my eyes adjusted to the dim light and re-

sponding to Watson's pull on the leash, I ventured farther into the barn. There, his leash hooked on to a piece
of alfalfa baling wire, was Bertie. He wagged his tail at
our approach and looked at me with those sorrowful
Basset eyes. Watson leaped forward to greet her friend.

"Hi there, Bertie," I said, forcing a cheerful tone and
unhooking the leash. "Where's the mister and missus,
then?" I didn't believe that, whatever the emergency that
had called Gert and Alf away at such short notice, they
wouldn't have taken Bertie with them. Or, if that wasn't
possible, at the very least they'd have locked him up
somewhere safe in the house. Something was very
wrong.

I was about to walk back out into the sunlight when
I heard a car approaching. Had the green monster arrived? Or was it Tony? I stayed out of sight and watched
through a crack in the barn door as one of those posh
Range Rover things came speeding down the dirt road,
narrowly missing the motor home and pulling up on the
driveway in a screech of gravel and dust.

I just had time to take in the 'Leo Fontaine, DVM,
Veterinarian to the Stars' emblazoned on the Rover's
side before a man jumped out. He was carrying something, perhaps a walking stick. It was difficult to see
from my angle. Had he come to see the ostriches? Could
I trust him?

I watched as he entered the house. After a few minutes
he came out again, looked at the motor home, peered
into my car, then went around to the back of the house.

I thought that it might be a good time to make my
getaway. With two large, bounding dogs—well, large,
anyway, they weren't pocket pets—I couldn't remain

hidden for long. I measured the distance with my eye and figured we could make it to my car before he came back around to the front of the house. I'd have to trust to luck that the car would start.

Taking a deep breath and a firm hold of both leashes, I stepped outside the barn and prepared to make a dash for it. And found myself looking down the business end of a rifle.

· 13 ·

The Intruder

Leo Fontaine, Veterinarian to the Stars, was the first to speak. "Who are you? What are you doing here?"

Determined not to let him see how scared I was, I pulled Watson closer to me and said, "I might well ask you the same thing. But I don't care who you are, you have no business entering the Pickles' house when they're not home."

He made no answer, but stood looking at me in amazement, and I continued, "Is it necessary to wave that gun around? Someone could get hurt. Do you really think you're in need of protection from a woman and two nonthreatening dogs?"

To my surprise, he lowered the rifle and started to laugh. Then, leaning the weapon against the barn wall he extended his hand in greeting.

"Leo Fontaine, the local vet. I'm looking for Mr. and Mrs. Pickles. Have you seen them?" His smile revealed small, expensively capped teeth.

Transferring the leashes to the hand with the catchpole, dropping Bertie's leash in the process, I shook his hand.

Gert had been right about the vet's looks. He was a handsome man, around six feet tall, with finely chiseled features, marred only by a slight weakness around the mouth. A smudge of grey in the well-trimmed dark brown hair, hazel green eyes. He was either blessed with great genes or spent a good many hours in the gym and paid close attention to his diet.

"Can I help you?" I said, hoping to convey by my manner that I was authorized to act as hostess in my friends' absence.

"We had an appointment," he said. "I was supposed to take another look at the ostrich."

Neither Alf nor Gert had mentioned a vet appointment. But it could easily have slipped their minds.

"If they're here, I haven't been able to find them yet," I replied. "But I only arrived a little while ago myself."

He allowed a puzzled look to cross his face. "I'm late. That's why I arrived in such a hurry." He smiled apologetically, as if trying to excuse his arrival in a cloud of dust.

I couldn't help myself. "Then why the rifle?"

He had the grace to look embarrassed. "There've been some coyote sightings recently. You can't be too careful with expensive livestock around."

Expecting to find coyotes in the house, was he?

The vet pulled on the knees of his tan boot-cut jeans and bent down to pet Watson. "Nice looking Dobie," he said. "Is it yours?"

The surest way to win me over is to admire my dog. I acknowledged ownership proudly, adding, "She has a really sweet disposition and gets along well with most people and with most other dogs, like with Bertie, here." I looked around for the Basset, but all I could see was the tip of his tail as he retreated into the barn. I wondered why he hadn't greeted the vet, whom the Basset surely would know well from the vet's frequent visits to the ranch.

"Do you know Bertie?" I tested.

"Oh, Bertie and I are old friends," he said. "It's probably too warm for him out here. He just wants to get into the shade." His eyes crinkled in a charming smile.

Watson seemed as taken with Dr. Fontaine as I was. She responded to the scratches under the chin with a tail wag and a nudge of the hand for more. Finally, I pulled her away. "She'll take that as long as you care to keep it up," I said.

He smiled. "Mind if I smoke?"

Before I could reply, he reached into an inside pocket of his suede jacket and pulled out an ostrich skin case from which he selected a cheroot and, striking a match on the sole of his boot, puffed it alight. He told me he lived on a nearby ranch, having recently given up his Hollywood practice in order to devote his time to his Las Vegas show-business clients and the local farm animals.

He may have been a newcomer to the ranching life, but he had fully embraced the Western mystique. From the top of his black Stetson hat with a silver plaited band, to the tips of his ostrich skin boots, he looked every inch the magazine ad cowboy. A colorful phrase of Howard's came to mind: "All hat and no cattle."

Even so, I might have been attracted to this very presentable man who could have been that rare creature who fit both Evie's requirements of a RNM and my own, but I had learned my lesson. I wasn't always the best judge of character when it came to men. We had only to consider my brief fling at matrimony with Roger to figure that out.

Besides, I liked my men a little less well put together, leaving some room for improvement, like Jack Mallory. No slouch in the dress department himself, Mallory nevertheless wore his clothes with the casual air of having just grabbed whatever came to hand. This urban cowboy gave the impression that a valet with a clothes brush hovered somewhere nearby.

I motioned to the Range Rover, the rear of which was filled with several varieties of potted plants. "You must be a plant fancier," I said, trying to match his cordiality.

He looked a little embarrassed. "It's an odd hobby, I know. But I'm redecorating and they give the place a lived-in look. I promised Mrs. Pickles I'd bring her some of my favourites the next time I visited."

"I'm getting really concerned about Alf and Gert. It looks like they left in a hurry," I said. "And it's just not like them to leave without Bertie. There must have been an emergency of some kind."

"I wouldn't worry. They probably had to go into town for something. They'll be back soon," he said. "They must have forgotten our appointment. When they get back, ask them to call the office to reschedule."

"I suppose," I said with less certainty, remembering the whistling kettle and the open front door. Not to mention my car, abandoned, the interior tossed. And what transportation did they use? They could have gone with someone else, of course. Willingly or unwillingly.

Dr. Fontaine broke into my thoughts. "What are you going to do?" He seemed impatient to be gone, yet at the same time reluctant to leave me alone. Was he concerned for my safety? Or perhaps he doubted my authority to be there. I ought to offer some sort of explanation.

"I'm an old friend of Alf and Gert's. I've been in Las Vegas and decided I'd take a side trip to see them. The name's—" I caught myself. I hardly knew this man, and despite his charm, something made me hold back. The rifle, no doubt. But, I reminded myself, this was the American West, and the presence of coyotes could be a real possibility.

But Posey's killers must have realized their mistake by now and could be looking for me. Maybe it was in the newspapers or on the radio. For the time being, it might be unwise to reveal my identity to strangers. Who knew but that Dr. Fontaine might unintentionally mention it to the wrong person?

Grasping for an alias, I remembered the stage-name game Evie and I used to play with our friends at school. You put the name of a childhood pet together with your mother's maiden name, with often hilarious results. I recalled a little white cat I'd had as a child. She had one blue and one green eye. She always insisted on using the bathroom window instead of the cat flap and, on her return, would do a high dive into the toilet any time someone forgot to put the seat down. Her name was— I stuck out my hand—"Kristal. Kristal Huggett," I said, adding my mother's maiden name. "My friends call me Kris. Perhaps Alf and Gert have mentioned me?"

He shook his head. "Where are you from?"

"England." That was true enough. I didn't have to say via Surf City, California.

"Ah. I thought I detected an accent," he said.

"I think I'll wait for them," I said. "They can't be too much longer."

I didn't want him to see me driving off in my car. So far, fortunately, he hadn't asked me how I got here. If I said the Country Squire, he might know better and wonder why I was lying. Admitting to driving the motor home would require a long explanation.

Besides, what would I tell him? It was all too unlikely a scenario, one I could scarcely believe myself, and certainly was not ready to confide to a man I had known for less than an hour.

"Miss Huggett," he smiled winningly, breaking into my thoughts. "Or may I call you Kris?"

I nodded.

"What I think you ought to do is to go back to Las Vegas and wait until you hear from your friends. You can leave them a note." He sounded very solicitous.

"I'm not leaving here without knowing what has happened to them," I said. "I think we ought to call the police."

"But then I would have to tell them I discovered you here alone. They might be suspicious. There would be endless questions and you'd be stuck here for hours. Me, too."

I hadn't thought of that. "But what about the ostriches and the other animals?"

"No problem. I'll send my vet tech out here later to take care of them."

We were interrupted by the ringing of his cell phone.

"Excuse me," he said with that charming smile. He threw down his cheroot, ground it into the dust with the toe of his elegant boot, and took his phone into the barn for privacy.

I waited patiently. There didn't seem to be much else I could do until he left, when I had every intention of calling the police.

"That was my office," he said. "Mr. Pickles called and asked them to relay a message to me apologizing for missing the appointment. They got called out of town unexpectedly."

I wondered again what vehicle they had used. Perhaps they had a second car. That would make sense. They wouldn't want to use the motor home all the time. But to forget Bertie? Something must have been terribly wrong for that to happen.

I was about to say so when we were interrupted by a sudden outburst of barking. It was coming from the direction of the ostrich paddock.

. 14 .
What's Up Doc?

WHO WAS DOING all the barking? Watson had never left my side. Bertie? The last I saw of him he'd slunk off into the barn. Where was he now?

Together, the vet and I made our way over to the paddock, where the ostriches, wings outstretched in attack mode, were chasing after a little Jack Russell terrier who alternately dodged and ran, then stood its ground in defiance, tail wagging, the effort of each bark lifting its front paws off the ground.

I knew that dog!

"Trixie!" I shouted. "Trixie, come here."

But the little dog seldom obeyed any voice but her master's, and Tony was nowhere in sight. In any case, at this point Trixie was probably far too excited to obey even him. Her total being was focused on the strange animals she found herself corralled with.

Dr. Fontaine had to raise his voice to make himself heard. "Do you know this dog?"

"Yes, I do," I shouted back. "Though what in the world she's doing here is beyond me."

I hurried over to the paddock, with catch-pole in hand, thinking perhaps that I might be able to use my erstwhile weapon for its intended purpose. The gate was padlocked, so I attempted to climb the chain link fence, but the vet pulled me down before I was halfway up.

"What do you think you're doing?" he said.

"I've got to get her out of there."

"She got herself in, she can get herself out again," he said. "As long as she doesn't get close enough to get kicked, she'll be okay. She'll tire eventually."

He was probably right. He'd had the experience. I suppressed a smile as I recalled Gert's story of the vet's encounter with Big Gus. Personal experience, then.

"I don't know," I said, still concerned. "I'm afraid she's going to get hurt if she stays in there."

While we stood there indecisively, we heard a whistle. The barking stopped immediately, and Trixie turned in her tracks toward the direction from which it had come.

Tony appeared from around the back of the barn. He strolled up to the paddock fence, whistled again, and the little dog, still barking, backed away from the ostriches, then turned, wriggled through a hole under the fence, and leapt into his arms.

"Who the hell are you?" demanded Dr. Fontaine.

"And a very good afternoon to you, too, mate," said Tony, drily. His eye travelled from the vet to the rifle leaning against the barn wall nearby.

Watson wagged her tail in greeting at two familiar friends. Bertie poked a tentative nose around the barn door.

"Tony," I said as the little terrier squirmed in his arms with delight. "I didn't know you knew Alf and Gert."

"Who? Me and Alf? We go back donkey's years. We was in the navy together." He winked at me. "Funny old world, ain't it?"

I wasn't the least sure he was telling the truth, but it wasn't a good idea to dispute the point in front of a stranger. On the whole, I was grateful to see a familiar face, though his timing might have been better. The fact was that invariably things got more complicated for me when my friends showed up, especially Tony.

The vet spoke up. "Kris, are you going to introduce me?"

"Kris?" said Tony, surprised.

"Oh, I know you usually call me Kristal," I said quickly, with a meaningful stare. "But I was telling Dr. Fontaine here"—a look of wariness crossed Tony's face—"that most of my friends call me Kris."

Tony twigged immediately. "Oh, right. Though I've always preferred Kristal meself." That was one good thing about Tony. I could always rely on him to be quick on the uptake. And to lie convincingly.

"Have you seen them? Alf and Gert?" I asked him. "I was supposed to meet them here, but there's no sign of them. From all appearances, they left in a hurry. Didn't even take their dog with them. I'm really concerned."

The vet's cell phone rang again. "Excuse me," he said, stepping back into the relative privacy of the barn. When he returned he seemed agitated. "I'm going to have to leave," he said apologetically. "Emergency at the clinic."

With a quick nod good-bye, he collected his rifle, hurried to the Range Rover, and drove off.

I watched as he sped down the lane, then turned to Tony. "Now would you mind telling me why you followed me here?" I was furious.

"Followed you? I'm just as surprised as you are."

"Don't give me that. I saw you."

"Saw me? Where?"

"On the road here. I saw you chasing after that green Corvette." A thought occurred. Maybe Tony wasn't alone. "Is anyone with you?" I asked.

"No. Who would be? I'm all on me Jack." That's Cockney rhyming slang for Jack Jones—Alone.

"Where's your car?"

"Back down the road, out of sight. I was following the cove in the Corvette, but he gave me the slip. I left Trixie in the car, but the little stinker must've wriggled out through the half-opened window."

Having had enough of the third degree, Tony took the offensive. "And what's all this about Kristal, then?"

"You almost let the cat out of the bag," I answered. "But you don't know what's happened. Or do you?"

Giving him the benefit of the doubt that he wasn't faking the blank stare, I told him of my telephone conversation with Jack Mallory. When I got to Posey's death, there was no question that his shock was genuine. With a pang I recalled how friendly he and Posey had seemed just the other day at my house, and I wished I'd broken the news more gently.

"Quite possibly in mistake for me," I continued. "Jack I mean Mallory, told me that the killers might be looking for me. So, when I met this total stranger, I thought it best not to give him my real name in case he mentioned it to someone else. Told him I was called Kristal Huggett."

"Kristal Huggett?" mused Tony. "Sounds like a bleedin' hooker. I'd expect you'd get in more trouble with a name like that than with your own. But it's wise not to tell everyone your business. And the way he took off out of 'ere . . ."

"Yes, in much the same manner as he arrived," I said. I told him how the vet had confronted me with the rifle.

His lips tightened. "See? What did I tell yer? Looks like I showed up just in time, then."

"I beg your pardon? I was handling things perfectly well until you appeared and nearly blew my cover."

"Oh yes, you was handling it, all right. He had a gun, didn't he? And why would a posh vet like that be doctoring farm animals, anyway? From what you say 'e 'as 'is 'ands full with all them fancy animal acts on the Strip. I'm not too sure about that bloke."

"And another thing," I added. "Alf and Gert said nothing about having a vet appointment this afternoon. Yet that's the reason he gave for being here." A thought occurred. "And now he's left without even looking at Big Gus."

"Who?"

"The sick ostrich."

"Didn't seem to be much wrong with 'im to me, the way he was chasing our Trixie around."

He was right.

My fears for Alf and Gert were mounting. "I borrowed their motor home for the night, so they drove my car," I explained to Tony. "By the time I got here, the wagon'd been torn apart, like someone was looking for something. Just like at my house." I came to a decision. "I'm going to call the police."

"But you said Dr. What's-is-name said they'd left a message at his office."

"I know. But why did they leave without Bertie, and

without turning off the kettle? I'll feel a lot better if I call the police. If I end up looking foolish, well it won't be the first time."

Tony shook his head. "You know how I feel about that. Don't ever involve the cops. The first one they'll suspect is you." Tony had an inbred distrust of the law, but was there some other reason he was reluctant to call the police?

"Now you're beginning to sound like Dr. Fontaine," I said. But he had a point. I would have to think this over.

"I tell you one thing," I said. "I'm not driving all the way back to Las Vegas without a cup of tea."

While Tony took Trixie to get his car, I headed for the kitchen, where I was sure I would find the makings of a decent cup of tea. Bertie and Watson padded along behind me.

I put the kettle on to boil and thought about what to do for the best. On an impulse I decided to call Mallory and ask his advice. Better do it before Tony got back. I picked up the kitchen telephone and dialled.

"Surf City Police Department." It sounded like Sergeant Bill Offley, Mallory's colleague. I'd always had the distinct feeling that he disapproved of me.

"Hallo. I'd like to speak to Detective Jack Mallory, please."

"He's out of the office."

"Is that Sergeant Offley? This is Delilah Doolittle. Is he likely to be back in the office soon?"

"Ms. Doolittle. Detective Mallory is out of town."

I couldn't hide my disappointment. "Oh. Is he on vacation?"

"We're not allowed to give out that information, ma'am." Sergeant Offley at his most officious.

"Thanks, anyway. Good-bye."

I hung up the phone just as Tony popped his head round the door. He showed no sign that he had overheard. "No chance of a cuppa, I suppose?"

"You're right. No chance." I was only half-joking. I was still mad at him. I knew he hadn't given me the whole story. Not now. And not two years ago.

But I soon relented. It was impossible for me to refuse a fellow countryman a cup of cha.

I stirred my tea thoughtfully.

"What's on your mind?" asked Tony.

"I'm still trying to make up my mind whether to call the local police."

Tony poured some tea into his saucer, blew on it, then placed it on the floor for Trixie. As I watched the little dog lap the warm, sugary brew, from the corner of my eye I thought I saw Tony brush something aside with his foot.

"Well don't do it before I'm clear of the place," he said. "I've 'ad more'n me share of run-ins with the old Bill."

Refreshed by the tea, we secured the house and prepared to leave. While Tony checked that my car was roadworthy I collected my carryall, Watson's kibble, and the cardboard box from the motor home.

When I placed the keys on the hook by the door, I had a closer look at the wall map of southern Nevada. I wanted to make quite sure I took the direct route back to Las Vegas. It was then that I noticed for the first time that there was a small inset map of what was obviously the Pickles' ranch. Noticed, too, the serial number printed at the bottom. It looked familiar. I took the deed out of my bag and compared numbers. Except for those missing on mine, they were identical. They were the same numbers that were scrawled inside the matchbook cover.

My mind took an impossible leap. The Pickles were raising ostriches on my silver mine! How could that be? Someone must have sold them the property illegally after Roger's death. But who? The suspicion that Alf and Gert were in on it and that their reappearance in my life had been no coincidence, I dismissed as soon as it occurred. No one would ever convince me that the Pickles were anything other than the dear, genuine, salt-of-the-earth types I had always believed them to be.

But there seemed no question that either I had the deed to the Pickles' property or the parcel adjacent to it. And that's what the thieves—the murderers!—had been looking for.

Now I could see the past more clearly than the present. The need both to find my friends and to learn how Roger had spent his last hours became more urgent with every new discovery.

I re-folded the deed, deciding that it was time to find a safe hiding place. I returned to my car and opened the cardboard box. Anybody interfering with this would regret it.

"You go on," I called to Tony. "I'm going to leave a note for Alf and Gert that I've taken Bertie with me, just in case they come back."

He waved and left.

I went back to the kitchen and found pencil and paper

by the telephone. I wrote that I had Bertie, gave every possible telephone number where I could be reached or a message left—my home number, Ariel's and Evie's, even, after careful consideration, Jack Mallory's at the Surf City PD—and assured Alf and Gert that I would take good care of Bertie until we met up again. Which I prayed would be soon.

It was no joke trying to lift a reluctant Basset hound, weighing almost as much as I did, into the back of a station wagon. I'd get the two front paws up on the tail gate, but before I could shove his rear end in, he'd turn around and wriggle down to the ground.

Watson looked on with interest, her head to one side.

"Don't just stand there. Give me a hand," I said jokingly when I paused to reassess the situation.

As if on cue, Watson obligingly jumped into the wagon. Immediately, Bertie clambered in after her, though not without a little assist from the rear—jumping not being his forte.

At the last minute, I remembered I should take some of Bertie's food with me. I had learned to my cost that it's not a good idea to make a sudden change in a pet's diet.

Back in the house, the first place I looked was in the cupboard under the sink. That's where I kept Watson's food at home. As I leaned down, I caught sight of a book of matches lying on the kitchen mat. I had one just like it in my carryall. It was from the Twilight Zone Motel.

. 15 .

Has Anybody Seen My Pals?

I WAS HALFWAY back to Las Vegas before I realized that Tony never had explained exactly what he had been doing at the ranch. I didn't believe that he knew Alf and Gert, as he claimed, nor that he had served in the British Navy with Alf. They had never mentioned him; never said they knew anyone in Surf City other than myself. More likely it was the first thing Tony had thought of to explain his presence at the ranch. Trusting to luck that neither the vet nor myself would know if Alf had, indeed, ever seen action in Britain's Senior Service.

Tony had taken off without telling me where he was going. I could make an educated guess, though. He must have spotted the matchbook cover when he gave Trixie her tea. Had he kicked it aside hoping I wouldn't see it? In an effort to keep me out of trouble? Or to put me off the scent?

I knew the matches weren't his. He didn't smoke. Neither did Alf and Gert. That didn't mean they might not have matches on hand for emergencies. But why matches from a seedy motel? Besides, Gert was a neat housekeeper. She wouldn't leave trash lying around.

No. Those matches had been dropped by someone else. Someone who frequented the Twilight Zone Motel.

Dr. Fontaine had been smoking his noisome cheroot, but one look at him and you knew he wouldn't be caught dead in a place like that. But that's where I last saw Roger, and that's where I was convinced I would find the answer to this mystery. And maybe Alf and Gert as well.

I turned on the car radio hoping to find some soothing music to calm my nerves. The strains of "Streets of Laredo" filled the air. I thought of my new acquaintance, the pseudo cowboy vet, and added a line of my own. "If I get an outfit can I be a cowboy, too?"

Dr. Fontaine was an attractive man, even if a bit over the top. Who arrives for an veterinary appointment carrying a rifle?

And what had happened to the driver of the Corvette?

Tony himself was not above suspicion. I was convinced he knew much more about the whole business than he was letting on.

WHEN I ARRIVED at the Twilight Zone Motel I found a large moving van blocking the driveway. From the illustration on its side of an angry-looking tiger jumping through a flaming hoop, I guessed it came from one of the casinos.

"I'd be angry, too, if I was forced to do such a dangerous trick," I said to Watson and Bertie, who had been roused from their dozing by the change in the car's rhythm after we left the freeway. "If Mother Nature had intended tigers to jump through flaming hoops, she would have given them asbestos coats."

The van's driver was nowhere in sight, so rather than wait indefinitely for his return, I turned around and drove half a mile back to a drive-thru chicken place I'd spotted on our way in. Buck-a-Cluck was not my dining experience of choice, but I was hungry. I had eaten nothing since the breakfast toast at the Lucky Hitch that morning. Even greasy fried chicken sounded good. Bertie and Watson would have enjoyed it, too. But I was much more particular about the dogs' diet than my own.

They had to be content with licking my fingers.

"You'll get your dinner when we're settled in the motel," I told them.

By the time we returned, the moving van had gone. I looked around for Tony's woody, but it was nowhere in sight. Maybe he'd stopped off somewhere. Or maybe he'd already arrived and taken off again.

The intervening years since I had last been there had not been kind to the Twilight Zone Motel. Its rating had dropped from third to fourth on my tolerance scale. The neon sign, vying vainly with the harsh glare of the late afternoon sunshine, flashed "Tw ight Zon. Vacancy." The sun-cracked red paint peeling from the unit doors added to the overall look of neglect.

The office door was warped, and I had to push hard to get it open. At least the air conditioning still worked, but an atmosphere of seediness prevailed. From the radio a country and western song whined something about a horse, a saddle, and a dog. I recognized it as one of Roger's favourites.

"We're full," said the sallow-faced desk clerk, without looking up. Fortunately, it was not the same chap as had officiated two years earlier. This one was dressed like a cartoon gambler—long-sleeved white shirt, bolo tie, a black vest, his greasy black hair slicked down on either side of a centre parting.

"The sign says 'vacancy,' " I countered.

Maybe it was my English accent that got his attention. He looked up and said, "Yeah. Well, it ain't working right."

I pointed out to him that there were very few cars in the lot. "Are you sure you don't have a vacancy? Please look again. I'm expecting to meet a friend here. Tony Tipton. Has he registered yet?"

He gave me an odd look. "Who wants to know?"

I looked over my shoulder to see if anyone was standing behind me. "I seem to be the only one here," I said.

"Just a minute." He went into a back room. Over the sound of the radio I could hear voices, low, male, possibly more than two of them.

He returned, followed by another man. It had been two years, and the lights had been dim, but I was certain that the ugly, heavyset man who accompanied the clerk was Roger's poker companion. The man Tony had called Lofty.

I don't think he recognized me. Other than Roger, Tony had been the only one who had looked directly at me that night. The other two had been far too intent on their card game.

Lofty stared at me for a moment or two, nodded to the clerk, then returned to the back room.

The clerk made a pretense of consulting the register, then, reaching behind him, took a key from the peg board on the wall and handed it to me.

Taking no chances, I signed the register Kristal Huggett.

As soon as I got to my room, I fed Watson and Bertie. Watson fell on her food eagerly. She must have been as hungry as I had been. But Bertie wouldn't eat. He was restless and kept scratching at the door.

"Missing mum and dad, are you?" I said, trying to calm him. "Never mind. We'll find them soon."

Later I took the dogs for a walk, looking for a quiet spot for them to do their business out of sight of the office and the other guests, if indeed there were any. In back of the motel, a small grove of trees, dusty in the early evening heat, offered the privacy we sought, and we made for the narrow path that ran between the trees and a large garagelike structure.

We had just started down the path when I noticed the rear end of a car partially hidden by the shrubbery. A car painted a bilious shade of green that could only be a certain Corvette. As we got nearer I could see the orange and yellow flames. There was no doubt about it. This was the car I had been accused of stealing on my previous visit to Las Vegas. The car I'd seen hurtling in the direction of the ostrich ranch earlier in the day. Did it still belong to the owner who had declined to press charges against me? It must. I didn't believe for a moment that it was just a coincidence that some newer owner was staying at the motel.

"Bertie, stop it. You're going to pull my arm off," I whispered to the Basset.

But Bertie, normally a docile dog who would do anything for a quiet life, kept pulling me toward the garage with an urgency there was no withstanding. When we reached the garage door, he just stood there and uttered a low, deep howl, a noise that I knew was the start of something bigger.

"Shh, Bertie. Please shh. You'll get us shopped."

But alternately scratching at the garage door and howling, Bertie refused to budge.

I looked around to make sure no one was watching, then attempted to lift the garage door with one hand. But the door was old and rusty, decrepit like everything else about the place. I had to attach the leashes to a nearby tree in order to have both hands free for the job. Finally, putting my shoulders into it, I was able to lift the heavy door open.

I collected the dogs, then, looking over my shoulder once more to make sure I was unobserved, I entered the building. The first thing I saw was Tony's woody. It was parked alongside a very large cage on wheels, the kind used to transport circus animals. It was enclosed on three sides and had a roll-up tarp cover in front.

My eyes adjusting to the gloom, I could see from the drag marks in the dust evidence that another, similar, cage had been there also. Been there quite recently to judge from the fresh-looking remains of the Buck-a-Cluck dinner wrapper Bertie was munching on.

. 16 .

Going Undercover

BUNDLING BERTIE AND Watson into the car, I headed for the Big Top Hotel. I had no clear course of action in mind other than a determination to find my friends.

All I had to go on was a hunch that they must have been taken away in the van that had blocked the driveway when I had arrived at the motel. What else would a casino vehicle of that size be doing at a dingy place like the Twilight Zone? They were probably being transferred at the very moment I was at the Buck-a-Cluck drive-thru. Why had it been necessary to move them? Did the kidnappers suspect that someone was on their trail?

How could this have happened? Though Tony was of slight build and in his seventies, he was as wily as they come. It would be hard to put something over on him unless the scales were unevenly balanced, like by a gun.

The Pickles were complete innocents and quite likely could have been tricked, though they would no doubt be very brave if put to the test. Their sheer size made them a formidable pair, certainly too large to be easily spirited away. Hence the cage. They would probably have been bound. Certainly gagged, for Gert would not be any better able to keep her mouth shut than under any other circumstances.

Unless, like Roger, they had been silenced forever.
But that I refused to believe, reassuring myself that they
must all still be alive. Otherwise, there would have been
no need for that cage.

And what about Trixie? She had to be okay, too. If
they had harmed her, she would have been left behind
in the garage.

AT THE BIG Top nothing seemed to have changed in the
two years since I was last there. The marquee still announced "The Busby Barkley Canine Chorus." The same
clowns picketed on the sidewalk, thrusting flyers at passersby. Or, if not the same ones, then others of their ilk.
As I watched them from the car park, an idea began to
form in my mind. Maybe they could help me infiltrate
the casino.

One of the clowns broke away from the crowd and
headed in my direction. Female, I guessed, from her
height and the large purse she was carrying. I got out of
my car as she approached. She took a flyer from her
purse and handed it to me.

"Hi," I said, taking the flyer. "As one animal lover to
another, I was wondering if you could tell me where I
could get a room where dogs are allowed." I nodded to
the two furry faces leaning out the car window, anxiously watching my every move.

As I had anticipated, Watson and Bertie proved an
irresistable attraction to this animal activist. "Hallo, poo-
chies," she said, reaching out and scratching their heads.
"Are you thirsty? Do you want a drink of water?"

I hastened to assure her that they were well fed and
watered, then went on to say, "I was here a couple of

years ago and saw your people protesting. I'm surprised you're still here."

She removed her red clown wig, revealing thick cropped brown hair. In her late forties, I guessed, her deep-set brown eyes showing the intensity of her commitment to her cause.

"It's a new audience every night," she explained. "Tourists. So we're educating people all the time. Maybe it doesn't have much impact on The Big Top's bottom line, but raising people's awareness is the most important thing. Most of the time, people just don't know any better. We give them something to think about."

She continued petting the dogs as she spoke. "Besides, we like to keep the spotlight on the shows. We have information that some of the dog performers were originally stolen pets."

I handed her my card. "That's why I'm here."

"Delilah Doolittle, PPI?" she read.

"Pet private investigator," I said smiling. "I'm working undercover, and I need to get in to rescue a pet I believe has been stolen."

I felt guilty about lying to this nice woman. But telling her more than she needed to know in order to enlist her aid could prove dangerous for her. Anyway, my story was almost true. It was exactly what I had done two years earlier. And I did need to get in to rescue Trixie.

"Trouble is," I said, "I need some place safe to stash these two while I'm busy. So if you could suggest somewhere—"

"I can do better than that," my new friend declared. "Come back to the office with me, and I'll fill you in. You can leave your car here. It's overnight parking for hotel guests." She took a sticker from her purse and slapped it on my windshield. "I knew this would come in handy some day," she grinned.

"I'm Judy," she said, helping me get Watson and Bertie out of the car. "Head cook and bottle washer of the A.R.M. protest. That's Animal Rescue Movement."

The office turned out to be a converted garage next to a ranch-style home in a residential section of the city. Our arrival was greeted by a flurry of poodles, who set up a barking frenzy every time someone arrived or left or, for that matter, dared to move.

A young woman, introduced to me as "one of our dedicated volunteers," stood at a copying machine running off brightly coloured flyers: EXPLOITATION IS NOT ENTERTAINMENT," "PUT THE A.R.M. ON ANIMAL EXPLOITERS." As soon as she saw Watson and Bertie, she left her post and reached for a box of dog biscuits on the top of a filing cabinet. I knew instinctively that my canine charges would be in good hands with these kind people.

At a desk in a corner of the room a man, whose name I was to learn was Harry, worked tirelessly at a computer. He was of indeterminate age and seldom spoke, keeping to his own mysterious business, only occasionally offering up a "ha" or an "uh-oh," upon coming across some especially heinous deed on the part of the opposition. It occurred to me that here was someone who might be able to help me with another aspect of this case that had been bothering me ever since I had left the ostrich ranch. I would have to find a chance to speak to him before leaving for the casino.

I sat down on a couch and was immediately pounced upon by an assortment of toy and mini poodles. One jumped into my lap, while two more ran across the back of the couch, sniffing my hair.

"All rescues," said Judy, punctuating her remarks with puffs on a cigarette. "From the Big Top. Poodles are the easiest to train, and those bastards will snatch 'em any time they can." I wasn't enchanted by her vocabulary, but had to admire her passion.

It must take a great deal of time and patience to train an animal, I thought. Surely it would be counterproductive for them to abuse their investment?

As if she'd read my mind, Judy took another puff of her cigarette and continued. "Even if they're treated well it's unnatural for animals to do tricks. It's even worse with the exotics."

She left the room and returned carrying a clown outfit. "Here, try this on," she said, handing me a shapeless yellow garment with green, red and blue balloonlike polka dots. "You can get it on over your clothes."

Indeed, since I was only wearing shorts and a T-shirt, that was no problem. The thing was huge. Definitely a one-size-fits-nobody kind of an outfit. It was comfortable, but I hoped its bagginess didn't impede my movements. I might need to act quickly tonight.

"Damn it!" said Judy as she helped me into it. "The fastener's broken. Wait while I get a safety pin."

Having adjusted the drooping neckline to her satisfaction, she sat me in front of a mirror and applied the face paint. Topped off with a rainbow wig, the disguise was complete. Even I didn't recognize myself.

"Now, what's your name going to be?" said Judy. "You're English. How about . . ." She thought for a minute. "How about Queenie?"

I was trying on a red foam rubber nose for effect when the door opened behind me. In the mirror, I saw a man dressed as a tramp clown in a ragged black suit, torn gloves, and a battered top hat with a daisy sticking out of it.

He wasn't wearing face paint, and I recognized him immediately. It was the sandy-haired card player. One-time, and as far as I knew, still associate of Lofty.

Had I walked into a trap?

· 17 ·
Punch

THE MAN DIDN'T RECOGNIZE me in my clown makeup. I don't think even my own mother would have. He'd only seen me that once, in a dimly lit motel room two years ago, but that night was etched forever in my mind. He was the short, sandy-haired man who had looked so gloomy at the card game when Roger was winning. He'd shaved off the wispy moustache, but if I'd needed proof, I had only to look at the tattoo on the back of his left hand—a heart enclosing the name "Judy."

I instinctively turned to Watson for backup, but she was staring at me in confusion. She wasn't at all sure if she knew the strange person with the rainbow wig and a big red nose.

Judy went up to the man and kissed him on the lips. "Punch, come and meet our new volunteer, Queenie."

I was thankful she didn't use my real name. I now regretted having given her the business card. I should have used my alias, Kristal Huggett.

Judy continued the introductions. "Queenie, this is Punch. We all go by code names here. We don't want reprisals. Judy's not my real name, either. Punch is our mole. He used to work at the casino, so he's a big help when we're planning a rescue, like tonight."

I nodded. I was afraid to open my mouth in case he recognized my accent. Did Judy know about his criminal background? But what did I know about it? Guilt by association was all I could accuse him of. That didn't mean he'd been a party to Roger's murder.

Besides, Judy seemed like a good judge of character. She'd taken me on, hadn't she?

Should I risk it and come clean? Nothing was what it appeared, including me in my clown outfit. Maybe I was the chief dissembler here.

I felt trapped. I stood up, making sure I had a clear path to the door. "I think I'll take the dogs for a walk," I muttered, reaching for their leashes.

"Not now," said Judy. "It's almost time to leave."

Punch, meanwhile, had walked over to the desk and picked up my business card.

"Perhaps this isn't such a good idea after all," I said, watching him. "I seem to be putting you people to an awful lot of trouble."

Before Judy could protest, Punch said. "Hold it right there, Delilah Doolittle. I thought I recognized that voice. You're Roger's wife."

My throat went dry. Fear prevented me from speaking. The only strength I had seemed to be flowing upward from the dogs through the two leashes. I had to stay calm for their sake.

"You two know each other?" asked Judy.

"We met a while ago," said Punch. "Remember I told you about a scam I was mixed up in? She's the wife of the guy who got killed."

Judy studied me with renewed interest. I knew I was expected to say something.

Finally I found my voice. "Did you have anything to do with that?" I asked Punch. There was nothing to be gained by pretending anymore.

Judy gasped in annoyance, and was about to protest, but Punch stopped her.

"No. I did not," he answered with a wry smile. "I got out of there right after you and that funny little English guy left."

Apparently Lofty had been losing all evening and wanted the chance to win back some of his money. "But he was tapped out," Punch explained, "and Roger wanted to leave." So Lofty had sweetened the pot. "Threw in the deed to some property he and some other guy were trying to scam. Said there was silver on it. Had a piece of ore right there in his hand." Punch shook his head. "He was so sure he had the best hand. Never expected Roger to win.

"After you left they started arguing again. Roger wouldn't give the deed back. I didn't like the looks of the way things were going, and I got out of there fast and never looked back. Never did know if they got the deed off of him. But when I heard his body had been found in the desert, I guessed what had happened."

So Roger had used me to get the deed out of the motel room. I remembered when he gave me the boots. He'd gone to the closet and had taken his time hanging up his jacket. He must have taken the deed out of his pocket and put it in the boot then. And got killed because he wouldn't tell where it was. I gasped. Had Roger died protecting me?

Tony was there that night. He would have known about the deed. And while he might not have known exactly what happened afterward, he was smart enough to have figured it out. When they didn't find the deed on Roger, did they suspect later that maybe he'd handed it to Tony to smuggle out of the motel room? Tony must have known trouble was brewing, and that was why he had been so eager to join me in my search for Lulu. I remembered how he'd seemed to be in a real hurry to get out of there.

Punch had said he didn't know if *they* had got the deed back. Had somebody else shown up after I left? I asked him. The other guy, maybe? Punch shook his head. Clearly, he'd said all he was going to on the subject.

While we talked, Judy had been on the phone rallying the evening contingent. They were to take up their positions at ten o'clock.

When Punch went to gas up the car, Judy told me how they had met. About two years earlier, after a confrontation with her outside the Big Top, he'd had something akin to a religious conversion and had joined A.R.M. A conversion of convenience, as it turned out, since he was on the run from both the law and his criminal associates at the time.

"I knew he'd gotten mixed up with a couple of guys running a real estate con," explained Judy, "and that something was weighing heavy on his mind. But I learned more about it tonight than he's ever told me before."

Deciding that honesty deserved honesty, when Punch returned, I told them my real reason for wanting to get behind the scenes at the Big Top.

"If your hunch is right," Punch said, "the only place

that would hold a cage that large, undetected, would be the storage area under the stage. It's hardly ever used because it's tough to get stuff out of there and upstairs to the stage. They use the warehouse out back for props now."

"How will I be able to get under the stage?" I said.

"Easy," he said. "In that outfit you'll blend right in. The whole place is done up like a midway. All the staff—the bouncers, security, cocktail waitresses— they're all dressed like circus people."

We proceeded to map out our strategy.

· 18 ·

Send in the Clowns

UNDER JUDY'S GUIDANCE, and with a nudge, I suspected, from Cupid, Punch appeared to have found his calling as an animal rights activist. They divided the leadership, with Judy taking the early evening and Punch the late shift.

With Punch in charge, our campaign started off with almost military precision. The fact that it did not end that way was due more to unforeseen circumstances than any lack of planning on his part. When dealing with animals, one always has to be prepared for the unexpected.

I was, I thought, completely unrecognizable in my clown costume. Even Watson still wasn't sure. She would stand gazing at me, her head cocked to one side, trying to understand, jumping back with an uncertain wag of her tail whenever I spoke to her. It was with reluctance that I bade her and Bertie farewell, despite Judy's assurances that she would guard them with her life—which I firmly believed she would.

Our transportation proved to be an ancient VW bus, bright yellow, decorated with red, blue, and green balloons. It was only slightly more roadworthy than a real circus clown car might have been, but just as colourful, and an equally effective attention-getter.

We made several stops along the way to pick up other protesters. By day they pursued traditional roles as homemakers, businessmen, and school teachers, but at night they united for a common cause, their clown outfits making them one jolly whole. We waited while a young mother kissed her toddlers good-bye, then we continued on to pick up a pharmacist, a used car salesman, and a hairdresser.

I tried to stifle my guilt at my subterfuge in using these dedicated volunteers as a cover. Wasn't I fighting crime and animal cruelty in my own way? And when Punch told us the dog to be rescued—a fawn Pug named Romeo—was performing in the Aida grand finale, I began to feel a real kinship with them all, recalling my own experiences in rescuing Lulu, Queen of the Nile. Though I might sometimes deplore their tactics I could not deny the righteousness of their cause.

As we neared the Big Top, Punch started to honk the horn, and opened the sunroof so we could stand up and wave at the passersby.

We parked across the street from the casino and Punch thrust a bunch of flyers in my hand.

"Give these out as you work your way to the entrance. I'll be watching. If you run into trouble, I'll create a diversion. As soon as you get the chance, duck inside. Once you're in, it'll be easier. Just try and stay clear of the strong men."

That was the first I'd heard about strong men. It didn't sound encouraging, but Punch was walking back across the street before I could get details.

The plan worked well at first. Handing out flyers right and left, I made my way to the entrance. But there I found my way blocked by a determined-looking carnival Strong Man, musclebound and bald, though I considered his flesh-tone tights detracting somewhat from the desired effect.

He grabbed at my shoulder as I attempted to pass through the door. "Hold it right there," he commanded.

I was about to turn and run when I heard the ear-shattering noise of a klaxon. I turned to see Punch riding a unicycle around the casino approach, tossing candy at the Strong Man as he went. Something like a jawbreaker found its mark. Mr. Musclebound let go of my shoulder and turned his attention to the cyclist. I dodged inside.

Punch was right. It was easy for me to blend in. The huge casino interior was designed as a three-ring circus, with slots and video poker machines in the centre ring; roulette wheel, craps, poker, and blackjack to one side; and a bar, lounge, and buffet section on the other.

Apart from the stone-faced dealers in their black pants and vests, white shirts and bolo ties, the casino employees were dressed in keeping with the circus theme. More Strong Men, I noted to my dismay. Security or bouncers, probably.

Weaving their way through the guests, dodging clowns, jugglers, and magicians at every turn, the cocktail waitresses balanced their trays with amazing ease and agility. They were dressed as ringmasters—though more well-endowed and buxom than most—their outfits of fishnet stockings, high heels, and low-cut, tightly fitted tuxedo vests leaving little to the imagination.

I had plenty of clown company and no one gave me a second glance, though whether the other clowns were part of the establishment or fellow protesters, I had no way of telling.

If there was music, it played unheard, drowned out by the rising and falling crescendo of the jangling slot machines, an endless *ker-ching*.

Everyone seemed intent on having a good time, all cares forgotten for a few hours in this Disneyland for grown-ups. In many cases the pervasive spirit of anything goes was reflected in choice of attire. Shorts and tees on the most inappropriate shapes and sizes mingled with the slinkiest of evening wear. For the women, especially, this was their chance to show off, to experiment. And they did, with often outrageous results.

One woman, certainly old enough to know better, was sausaged into a harlequin leotard that fit only too well like the proverbial glove. A white ruff circled her neck. In one hand she carried a small black satin purse. Over her eyes she held a black mask on a wand. If an air of mystery had been the desired effect, it was somewhat marred by the fact that she had trouble seeing where she was going, as she tottered on high-heels from the roulette table to the wheel of fortune. As a humble clown, I began to feel almost unobtrusive amid such flamboyance and began to relax.

Always a danger for someone working undercover.

Overhead, high-wire acts balanced with breathtaking grace, and trapeze artists swung perilously to and fro, risking life and limb. Ignored, certainly unappreciated for the most part by the visitors below, who were intent only on the big win.

I was so busy watching the daring stunts overhead that I didn't look where I was going, with the consequence that I bumped into someone. It was the harlequin woman.

"Oh, I'm so sorry," I said.

"Delilah!" Evie's cut-glass tones pierced the din. "I've been looking for you everywhere!"

· 19 ·

Luck be a Lady

"MY DEAR, WHERE *have* you been? You gave us such a scare. For a few hours we all thought you were dead." Evie raised the mask to her eyes and peered at me. "You might just as well be if you're going to go around in that absurd outfit."

Talk about outfits! This wasn't exactly her finest fashion hour, either.

She had to speak at the top of her voice to be heard over the casino din, and it seemed to me that every head in the place turned in our direction.

"Evie, please keep your voice down," I said in what I hoped was a whisper. "I'm here undercover." How daft that sounded.

She echoed my thought. "Undercover of what? Oh I get it. Well, that's quite ridiculous. I recognized you the moment you opened your mouth."

"Look. We can't talk here. Let's go and have a drink." I took her arm and led her toward the cocktail lounge.

I was all for sinking into one of the comfortable upholstered arm chairs, but Evie chose to perch, or rather lean, on a stool at one of those little round tables beloved by cocktail bars.

"Can't sit in this outfit," she confided. "In fact, I can scarcely move."

"Then why wear it?" The words were out of my mouth before I realized I was hardly in a position to criticize, considering my own costume. But I didn't apologize. I was getting edgy. Evie's presence was a complication I could have done without.

Perhaps a drink would settle my nerves. We ordered two gin and tonics. "Oh, and a packet of ciggies, too, sweetie," Evie instructed the astonished ringmasterette. "Sobranies if you have them. Otherwise, whatever you've got."

While we waited for our drinks, I asked her how she came to be there. "The Big Top's hardly to your taste."

She reached into the tiny black clutch and took out a telescoping cigarette holder and a small silver lighter and placed them on the table.

"It's Howard, sweetie. He's here on business, and he has a teensy share in the place. So we get a discount."

Funny how the rich are always on the lookout for a bargain. That's how they stay rich, I suppose.

"I've told Howard he has to sell out. I can't bear to watch those animal acts. Give me the Cirque du Soleil any time. Did you see those clowns demonstrating outside?" Light dawned. "Oh, I say. That's not your case, is it? Are you going to do something excitingly subversive, like blow up the place? Do me a favour, sweetie, and wait until Howard sells."

The waitress returned with our g&t's and a pack of Marlboros. Evie charged the drinks and the cigarettes to her room then, after inserting a cigarette into the holder, she continued. "But wait. I must tell you that I have been through the most appalling experience on your account. I went to your house—you know, I did let you know I was coming, left a message on your machine—and you weren't there. But I thought you *were*. Anyway, I looked in the window, and I saw, well—" she took a dramatic pause "—what I saw was a very dead body. Yes, I tell you she was dead. No question about it. I thought it was you! I nearly had a heart attack. It really is most inconsiderate of you not to consider your friends' feelings a little more. I was quite hysterical, had to call the police, and be interviewed and everything. It turned out that it was the woman next door. I told you it was an unsavoury neighbourhood the moment you moved there. I knew no good would come of it."

Oh lord, I hoped she wasn't getting wound up to start badgering me about moving again.

She finally paused to take a sip of her drink, and I encouraged her to keep to the topic at hand. "And then what happened?"

"Well, that policeman boyfriend of yours, detective somebody or other, showed up."

"Jack Mallory. Yes, I know all about it. I've spoken to him on the phone. And he's not my boyfriend."

"Yes. Mallory. That's right. Well, believe me, dear, I wouldn't have thought he had it in him, but for a while there when we all thought you were dead, he was almost as upset as I was. His face was drained, darling. Absolutely drained."

Anguished at having been the cause of so much suffering to my friends, I pressed for more details. "What did he do?"

"Well, after what seemed an interminable time, he came over to Ariel's house—what a sweet woman!—to tell me they'd identified the body—it wasn't you, thank

God—and that you were staying in Vegas somewhere. Of course, I couldn't rest until I'd seen you with my own eyes. Howard was already here on business, so I flew here with the policeman."

My heart missed a beat. "Jack—Mallory's here? In Las Vegas?"

"Yes."

Mallory's presence would be very comforting right now. "Where is he?"

"How should I know? Not here, one would hope. He was absolutely the worst company on the plane. A complete bore. Barely spoke two words the entire trip. But never mind about him." She leaned forward and lowered her voice. "You got my message? About that Nevada property of Roger's?" I nodded. "Well, Howard's done some checking, and it turns out that it wasn't legally Roger's in the first place. Which we might have guessed. He's supposed to have won it in a card game, or some such nonsense."

A card game! That must be the one he played in the night he died. It was extremely unlikely that there had been two such occasions on which he'd won or lost the deed to somebody else's property.

Evie broke into my thoughts. "There still seems to be some question about the deed, but that's all Howard was able to find out." She leaned over and patted my arm. "Sorry to disappoint you, sweetie."

Before I could tell her that none of this was exactly news to me, she looked around as if concerned that we might be overheard, then said, "Never mind. The best is yet to come! I have found you the absolutely most perfect man! Actually, he's a part owner here and is the one who's interested in acquiring Howard's share. He's just waiting to complete another business venture to liquidate some capital. As RNM go, you couldn't do better if you made up a pattern. He's rich, divinely good-looking, and to top it all off, what do you think?"

"I have no idea."

"He's a vet! Now what could be nicer for you? I tell you my dear, it's a perfect match. And he's here now. I was talking to him not an hour ago." She looked across the bar to the poker tables in the adjacent arena. "There he is. Yoo hoo, Dr. Fontaine!"

I gasped. What in the world was *he* doing here? But Evie was right. He did have possibilities. Could she have finally come up with the right RNM?

Evie obviously misinterpreted my reaction. "I warn you, if you're going to say something crushingly sensible, I shan't listen."

"No. I was simply going to say . . ."

Impatiently, Evie tapped her cigarette into the ashtray. "I know, sweetie. It's unfortunate he lives in Las Vegas. But there, one can't have everything."

On hearing her call out, Dr. Fontaine had looked up and nodded, but mercifully did not seem inclined to leave his card game. I was not exactly dressed for courtship.

Evie echoed my thought. "Just as well. Wouldn't do to have him see you in that appalling getup. First impressions, etcetera." Raising her lorgnette, she took a hard look at my rainbow wig. "And, for goodness sake, sweetie. You're going to have to do something with your hair!"

That mask wasn't doing much for her vision.

I didn't let on to Evie that Dr. Fontaine and I were already acquainted. She would insist on knowing details. It would take too long to explain. Besides, I didn't want to steal her thunder.

I got up to leave. "I'll meet him some other time, luv. I'll catch up with you later. I told you I'm working on a case right now, and people's lives could be at stake."

"Really, Dee. Must you be so melodramatic. I suppose it's another one of your lost-dog efforts."

"No. Much more serious."

I'd already told her too much. I didn't even know for sure Tony, Alf, and Gert were on the premises. They were proving harder to find than fleas on a black cat.

"Sit—I mean, stand tight," I told Evie. "If I'm not back in half an hour, come looking for me in the storage area in the basement. Under the stage. And keep an eye out for Tony. If he should show up, bring him with you."

"Tony? *He's* here too? How is the dear boy?"

"Not doing so well at the moment. I'm afraid he might be in a lot of trouble. That's why I'm here."

I left her, for once speechless. Fortified by the g&t— Dutch courage some would call it, but I'd take my courage where I could find it, and I've always found the Dutch to be agreeable folk—and following Punch's directions, I made my way to the basement. Nobody tried to stop me. More people were in regular clothes behind the scenes, but there were still enough in costume that I did not look conspicuous.

Eventually I came to a door that opened onto a narrow stairway, leading down to a dimly lit passage criss-crossed with exposed plumbing, ductwork, and insulation. There was no air-conditioning down there, and the

air was musty and claustrophobic. The noise, so deaf-
ening in the casino, was reduced to no more than a muf-
fled hum.

I was beginning to think that Punch had been mistaken in guessing this would be the hiding place and
was about to retrace my steps when I heard voices. One
of them was Tony's.

"Come on, mate," he was saying. "Let's be reasonable
'ere."

A man's voice, harsh and unyielding, answered, "We
are being reasonable. It's simple enough. The boss says
if they sign over the property, they'll get the dog back."

What dog? Trixie? Who was the boss? Punch hadn't
told me. He was too scared. I got closer to the door,
trying to catch every word.

Then I heard Gert's voice. She was sobbing. "Please,
we'll do anything. Please don't hurt our Bertie."

I drew a sharp breath. The swine was pretending he
had Bertie stashed away somewhere and was threatening
to kill him.

Alf, more pragmatic, tried to strike a bargain. In his
north country accent, slow and ponderous, he was saying: "We can't do that. It's our living. We can pay you.
We've got the brass. Just let us out of here so we can
get to the bank."

"Or go to the police," sneered the voice. "No way
you're getting out of here without signing. You've got
an hour to think it over. Or it's bye-bye Bertie."

The door opened and I hurriedly ducked behind a
packing crate. Immediately I recognized the dark, heavyset man who emerged. It was Lofty.

As soon as I heard the door at the top of the stairs

close behind him, I came out of my hiding place and entered a large storage room that appeared to be almost directly under the stage. A canvas chute, similar to those used by airlines in emergencies, hung from what I guessed was a trapdoor. To the far side of the room were large double doors through which the cage holding my friends must have been brought in.

Tony, Gert, and Alf were sitting on the cage floor, their hands and feet bound. Trixie sat in Tony's lap.

They didn't know who I was at first, and Trixie kept up a constant yapping until I removed the wig and the red nose. Their astonishment on recognizing me was followed by concern that I had been tailed and would be captured along with them.

The first thing I did was to reassure Gert and Alf that Bertie was in safe hands.

"But how did you know where we were, luv?" asked Alf.

"No time to go into that now," I said. "We've got to get you out of here."

With Trixie still cradled in his lap, Tony scooted his way over to me and thrust his hands through the bars of the cage so I could untie them. He, in turn, released Gert and Alf.

The cage gate was padlocked. We would have to pick the lock.

"Piece of cake," said Tony, handing Trixie to Gert. "Give us a hair pin."

Neither Gert nor I had a hair pin, and I had nothing about my person that we could use instead. My carryall contained all kinds of odds and sods that might have come in handy. But my carryall was back at Judy's house.

Then I remembered the safety pin Judy had used to secure the neck of my clown suit. I reached back and gave it to Tony. Unfortunately, with the pin's release the suit slipped down around my shoulders, hampering my movements. All in a good cause, I shrugged, trying to fashion the fabric into some kind of a knot. But I could tell by the frustration on Tony's face that the pin wasn't adequate to the job.

It was taking too long.

"It's no good," I said finally. "I'll have to go and get help." With luck, I might run into Punch.

Tony had straightened up from his task and was nodding his head, indicating that I look behind me. "Why? What's the matter?"

I turned as a familiar voice said, "Not to worry, darlings. Evie to the rescue."

With her was my RNM du jour, Dr. Leo Fontaine.

• 20 •

Don't Bother, They're Here

LEAVE IT TO Evie to make matters worse. Dr. Fontaine was one complication I could have well done without. I felt embarrassed and at a disadvantage in the clown suit, especially since I was sure Evie had given me quite a buildup, and he would be expecting someone presentable, if not outstanding. Certainly not Queenie the Clown. Or even Delilah Doolittle, come to that. He knew me as Kristal Huggett. I trusted that Evie had so far only referred to me as "my friend."

His greeting was all charm and good manners. "So, Miss Kristal Huggett. We meet again."

Evie gave a nervous little laugh. "Kristal who? Wherever did you get that from? It must be that ridiculous costume she's wearing. This is the friend I've been telling you about. Delilah Doolittle."

Tony ran his hand down his face and uttered a hushed, "Oh, my gawd."

The vet looked at me in surprise. "Delilah Doolittle? I thought you were dead."

Evie, probably beginning to realize that there was more going on than she was privy to, looked a little peeved. "So did we, darling," she said. "Fortunately, or unfortunately, depending on one's point of view, of course, it was the woman next door who was killed in Delilah's house."

The vet looked confused, shocked, and angry all at the same time. Though whether because I wasn't dead or because he'd been taken in by my alias was hard to tell.

In any event it was too late to deny my true identity. "How did you know I was supposed to be dead?" I asked him.

"I must have read it in the newspaper or seen it on television," he answered.

That didn't sound very likely. With murders a daily event in many U.S. cities, news of the killing of one insignificant person in Southern California would not be very likely to make even the back page of the Las Vegas papers, never mind television.

All this time Alf and Gert had been looking from me to Evie to Dr. Fontaine and back again in amazement.

Gert, who was still holding Trixie, peered through the cage bars at the vet. "Well, I never," she said. "Who would have thought we'd run into you here, Dr. Fontaine."

"Yes, sir," said Alf. "It's real nice of you to come and give us a hand."

Evie, seeming to catch sight of Tony for the first time, approached the cage.

"Tony, my dear boy. Whatever have you been up to, caged there like a wild beast?" She regarded Alf and Gert with interest. "Won't you introduce me to your friends?"

Our attention was diverted momentarily when, from the stage overhead, came the sound of the Triumphal March. I could imagine the scene: the poodle chorus line, the gondola drawn by the golden retrievers, and the Pug enthroned where Lulu had once sat in all her glory. We all looked up.

All, that is, except Dr. Fontaine. Taking advantage of the distraction, he grabbed my arm. I tried to pull away, but he held it in a tight grip.

"You're trying to play me for a fool, you little—" he said, using language I don't care to repeat. "Where's the deed your husband stole from me?"

"Stole?" I said in disgust. "From what I hear, he won it in a card game." I should very much liked to have given the vet a piece of my mind, but it's hard to be dignified in a floppy clown suit.

The music overhead was now mingled with the sounds of scuffling and, it seemed, raised voices.

Evie's eyes darted from one to another of us. While not in total grasp of what was going on, she was, I guessed, waiting for an opportunity to come to my assistance. But her options were somewhat limited, her movements hampered by the harlequin leotard.

Her tongue, however, was under no such restriction. "I say," she said to Dr. Fontaine. "I'll thank you to treat my friend with a little more courtesy. We English are not accustomed to such coarseness."

The vet's response to that was to grab her with his free hand and start to hustle us both toward the door.

At that precise moment, Tony, who had been furtively working on the padlock all along, finally got it sprung, flung the cage door open with a clang and, before Fontaine knew what was happening, raced over and jumped him from behind.

Together, Tony, Evie, and I shoved the vet into the

cage. Alf knocked him down with a thump, and Gert sat on him while Tony tied him up with the rope that had been used on the captives earlier. Trixie, who Gert had put down at the start of the punch-up, yapped the whole time from a safe distance.

Alf helped Gert to her feet and gave her a hug. Evie hugged Tony, and I picked up Trixie and hugged her. In fact, we were all so busy hugging one another that we were unaware the storage room door had opened until we heard a man's voice and turned to see Lofty standing there, a gun at the ready.

"Everybody on the floor," he commanded.

Evie was the first to speak. "In this outfit? You must be joking."

But Lofty was quite devoid of humour. "You heard me," he snarled.

Holding to the side of the cage for support, poor Evie slithered to the floor. The rest of us gathered around her in defeat. Trixie was the only one to take the offensive. Leaping from my arms she charged Lofty's pant leg, tugging at it in true terrier fashion. He shook her off with a curse, and she retreated to Tony's feet. Tony put up his fists ready to do battle, but there really wasn't much he could do, confronted with an angry gunman.

Keeping one eye and the gun on us, Lofty edged over to the cage and released Dr. Fontaine.

"About time you showed up," the vet snarled, shaking his shoulders and smoothing the sleeves of his jacket. "Maybe you can persuade Mrs. Doolittle here to tell us where the deed is."

Trixie, meanwhile, was back on her feet, and with

slightly less energy, but still as much determination, made another rush at Lofty's pant leg.

He pointed the gun at Trixie. "Tell us where the deed is, or the dog gets it." There was no mistaking his tone.

He then turned the gun on me. "I mean it!"

Evie screamed. "Delilah. For God's sake. Tell this madman what he wants to know."

"All right, Mrs. Doolittle," said Fontaine. "You heard your friend. Where is it?"

I had no choice. "It's—it's in my car. In the parking lot. The Country Squire wagon. You should be able to recognize it by now."

Tony shook his head sadly. "Sorry, luv," he said, picking up Trixie, who finally seemed to appreciate the seriousness of the occasion.

Fontaine took the gun from Lofty, and with a nod of his head, indicated that his partner should go and fetch the deed.

"What are you going to do with us?" asked Evie.

"We're going to wait here until he gets back, to make sure she's telling the truth, then we're all going for a little ride in the desert," the vet replied.

"Look here," said Evie. "I'm not dressed for this kind of thing, and I've had just about enough of you. Must you be so bloody-minded? If you think my husband is going to sell you his shares in the casino after this, you've got another think coming."

"Oh, I don't agree. I think he'll be very cooperative when he knows just how high the stakes are," he answered, with a menacing wave of the gun.

While we were gloomily mulling over the portent of his words, the noise overhead had reached a crescendo.

Suddenly there was a crash, a snap, as of wood breaking, and the stage trapdoor burst open. Punch, a fawn Pug, presumably Romeo, clutched tightly in his arms, came tumbling down the chute. He was immediately followed by a motley assortment of other clowns and canines.

A standard poodle chancing to charge the vet from behind, caused his knees to buckle. The gun flew from his hand and was ably fielded by Alf.

"Well caught, sir!" said Tony in parlance reminiscent of England's cricket fields.

Once again Dr. Fontaine found himself on the wrong side of the cage bars.

Clowns were everywhere. Tumbling on top of one another as they landed at the bottom of the chute, stopping to help each to his or her feet, getting knocked down again as more arrived. Though their plan, whatever it had originally been, had not been entirely successful, they seemed not in the slightest bit daunted as they rapidly tried to round up the pooches running amok in the storage room.

The mood dampened quickly, however, when distant sirens heralded the imminent arrival of the police.

Still holding tight to the Pug, its moist eyes bugging in bewilderment, Punch headed for the large double doors. "Come on! This way!" he called.

Alf and Gert, after a quick nod from me assured them that they would be in good hands, were only too ready to obey, but Tony hesitated. Encumbered with Trixie, who had jumped into his arms the minute she heard the sirens, he was trying to help Evie to her feet.

"Go, Tony," I said. "I'll look after Evie. We can't risk you getting arrested. Not with your rap sheet."

"But I can't leave you 'ere, luv," he said.

"Listen. If you get arrested, Trixie will end up in the pound. And someone's got to make sure Alf and Gert get away safely. I'll be okay. Go. You too, Punch." It wouldn't do for him to get arrested, either. Besides, he had to get the Pug back to its owner. What's more, once his cover was blown, he would be in real danger from his former associates. They would know he could testify against them if the investigation into Roger's death was reopened. As far as I could tell, Fontaine hadn't yet recognised him in his clown suit.

"Meet up back at the house," Punch called over his shoulder to me as he hustled Tony, Trixie and the Pickles through the double doors.

I helped Evie to her feet. She didn't appear in the least concerned at the prospect of being arrested.

"What are they going to arrest *me* for? I have absolutely no idea what any of this is about. It's obviously another of your shameful escapades, Delilah, and I trust that when the time comes, you'll give me a proper explanation. But I, personally, have nothing to fear from the police."

She turned and glared at the vet. "As for you," she snapped. "I intend to file charges for assault and battery. Not only that, I'll—" she groped for words "—I'll have your license. You've no business handling defenseless animals."

"Shut up," he muttered, all amiability drained from his face. That had been an act, I realized now, and one that had probably cost quite an effort to maintain. I wondered that I had ever thought him attractive.

By now, trainers and showroom staff had arrived by

the more conventional stairway and were gathering up loose poodles and retrievers.

"Come on, Evie," I said, tugging on her arm. "No time for that now. The police will take care of him. They'll be arriving any minute."

And arrive they did. And very soon thereafter, both Evie and I were under arrest.

"On what charges, may I ask?" demanded Evie.

"How about false imprisonment, for a start?" said the policeman, nodding his head in Fontaine's direction. "Then there's disturbing the peace, demonstrating without a permit, breaking and entering, dog theft, and—" he added as Evie went to bop him over the head with her tiny handbag—"assault on a police officer in the performance of his duty."

"You've got it all wrong," I protested. "This man here is the one guilty of kidnapping and imprisonment." I realized this statement lacked a certain credibility even as I said it, considering that Fontaine was the one now behind bars. But I soldiered on. "He has kept our friends incarcerated, trying to coerce them to hand over their ranch to him."

The policeman looked sceptical. "Where are these friends of yours? Why aren't they here to press charges?"

Of course, by this time, Tony, Alf, and Gert had got clean away.

Released from the cage, Fontaine thanked the policeman and was preparing to be on his way, too. But the officer insisted he also accompany him to the station.

"We'll need everybody's statement, and we'll sort it all out there," he said, holding the vet firmly by the arm.

A large crowd clogged the sidewalk, jostling for a good look at the strange sight of a bunch of clowns being herded into a paddywagon by more than twenty police officers, many of them in riot gear. Some of the bystanders no doubt thought it was all part of the Big Top's show.

Evie was having trouble keeping her balance on her high heels as the police hurried us through the crowd. I tried to help her, but I was having difficulty myself. The clown suit kept slipping off my shoulders and would have likely fallen around my feet if I hadn't held it bunched up at my waist. All was a blur of clowns, picket signs, leaflets, policemen, and gawkers. But I do distinctly remember the last face I glimpsed before being handed into the paddywagon.

It was that of Detective Jack Mallory.

• 21 •
Busted!

"DELILAH DOOLITTLE, AKA Kristal Huggett, aka Queenie the Clown," read the detective in charge. Young, crew cut, thin, he smelled of aftershave, and looked as if he spent many hours at the gym. According to the plastic ID on his shirt pocket, his name was Davidson, J. "Demonstrating without a permit, false imprisonment, dognapping—"

"Hang on a tick," I said, bristling. "What dog am I supposed to have 'napped?"

He consulted his notes. "A Pug, male. Answers to the name of—"

"Stuff and nonsense," I interrupted. "I know nothing about any such animal." Though I certainly did and hoped that Punch had restored Romeo to his rightful owner by then.

"You could be looking at six months in jail."

"For what?" I said, vainly trying to hold on to my dignity while grasping the folds of my oversize costume around my waist. I had been offered a chair, but I was too upset to sit down. "About the only thing I might justly be accused of is wearing this ridiculous garment in public. And if peculiar clothing is against the law, then half the people in Las Vegas should be in jail."

Unperturbed, the young detective continued reading from a manila folder. "Priors, grand theft auto two years ago. A Corvette."

Evie, who had been listening in open-mouthed amazement, could contain herself no longer. "This is an outrageous abuse of power," she declared. She took her cell phone from the tiny purse—surely the last item she could possibly have stuffed in that dainty receptacle—and started viciously stabbing at the key pad with a well-manicured finger. She was trying to reach Howard. "He's not there?" she said impatiently into the phone. "Well, for God's sake where is he? Find him and tell him to come to the police station straightaway. It's a matter of life and death."

I hoped it wasn't that bad.

Ignoring the interruption, the detective turned to Dr. Fontaine and, in a deferential manner that made my blood boil, said, "It says here that you dropped the charges in that case, sir."

I looked at the vet in amazement. "It was you?" Memories of that day at this same police station two years earlier came flooding back. I had come to report Roger's disappearance and had wound up instead being accused of stealing the Corvette. I recalled how puzzled I'd been at the time that the charges had been dropped by the anonymous owner. Fontaine had been dogging my footsteps even then.

Now it was clear he must have lent Roger the car, then once Roger was dead, had reported it stolen as the easiest means of getting it returned to him.

"Car theft! Delilah! Impossible! There must be some mistake. She can't even *drive* a Corvette, never mind *steal* one. Besides, my friend is a woman of the utmost integrity. It's a case of mistaken identity. Tell them, Dee. Tell them that you never set eyes on that, that, so-called vet, until this week."

She didn't know the half of it.

I was truly scared. If found guilty as charged, I might be sent to prison, even deported since my marriage to Roger had conveyed only resident alien status, not citizenship. If released, I felt sure that Dr. Fontaine would not rest until he'd had me done in. I knew too much. He wouldn't do it himself, of course. No, once again he would send his henchman to do his dirty work, and this time there would be no Posey to be mistaken for me.

My friends would do all they could. But their all would amount to very little once they found themselves dodging the vengeful vet. He obviously believed he had nothing to fear from the law. He'd got away with Roger's murder, hadn't he?

My spirits picked up when Evie's husband Howard arrived accompanied by their attorney, Max Oberon. In no time, they had Evie released from custody, having persuaded the casino management to drop the charges against her. That had been easy enough. She had been held on suspicion of being my accomplice, but there was no evidence that she was guilty of anything except being in the wrong place at the wrong time.

Things were different in my case. I wasn't about to get off so easily.

At Evie's insistence, Howard and Max once again manned their cell phones to do some string-pulling. Eventually, after what seemed like an interminably long time, during which I was booked, fingerprinted and photographed, Howard and Max returned with some news.

"The casino is prepared to drop the charges if you will give them information about the animal activists. The identity of their leader is especially important to them. They have been trying to break up this ring for years, for disrupting performances, stealing animals, and giving the Big Top a poor image."

"A poor image," I sniffed. "I think they've managed to acquire that all by themselves."

Nobody appeared to have a ready response to this, so I continued, "I certainly have no intention of ratting on my friends. I'm no clay pigeon." The detective tried to hide a grin at the slip of the tongue. "You can deport me if you must, or put me in your darkest dungeon, feed me bread and water, but—"

"Don't forget pulling fingernails," said a familiar voice.

He must have just arrived. Or had he been there the whole time, unobserved? Embarrassed though I was that he should find me in such a predicament, and looking such a sketch at that, I could not disguise my pleasure at seeing Jack Mallory. I'm sure it was betrayed in my voice. "Why, Jack! What are you doing here?"

He patted my shoulder gently, then took a seat by the detective's desk. "Never take up a life of crime, Delilah," he said wryly. "You leave a trail a blind man could follow."

Except for the affection in his tone I might have taken offense at that. But I was so pleased to see him, I chose not to.

Belatedly realizing that there was no longer any point in maintaining my clown disguise, and that I was still wearing my shorts and T-shirt underneath, I let go the folds of fabric and the suit fell around my feet. With as much dignity as I could muster, I stepped out of the offending garment, folded it, and placed it over my arm.

While Detective Davidson talked to Howard and Max, Evie's staccato pitch intruding into the conversation anytime one of the three men paused to take a breath, and Dr. Fontaine lounging in the only comfortable chair in the room, puffing on a cheroot, Mallory took me aside and explained his presence there. His investigation into Posey's murder had led him to Las Vegas, and the information he shared with the local police had caused them to reopen their file on Roger's death.

He turned to Fontaine and showed him a photograph. What I believe in police jargon is called a mug shot. "Do you know this man?"

The vet blew a smoke ring. "Never saw him before in my life."

I looked over Mallory's shoulder. The picture was captioned BUD FLETCHER, but I recognized the swarthy, heavyset man immediately. It was Lofty.

"Don't you believe him," I said to Mallory. Then, my voice raising in anger, I turned to the vet.

"How can you say you don't know him? That man was there with you, in the casino basement tonight, bullying Mr. and Mrs. Pickles to hand over their ostrich farm and threatening to shoot a defenseless dog."

The argument brought Davidson, Howard, and Max over to us.

"Lies. All lies," Fontaine blustered. "She had her accomplice,"—he nodded at Evie—"lure me to the casino basement, where she and her gang,"—here I heard a gasp from Evie, and a smothered chuckle from Mallory and Howard—"forced me into the cage and threatened me. Fortunately, the police showed up soon afterward, or I might not have lived to tell about it."

Davidson wrote it all down.

"Oh, for heaven's sake," I said, "Why would I need to do that? He's the one who's telling lies. Ask him who killed Posey Brightman in my house."

"Never heard of the woman," Fontaine replied. "And I can prove I wasn't in California at the time."

"What time was that?" put in Mallory. He had him there.

"No, you probably weren't," I chimed in. "It's your accomplice who will have to take the drop for that. I hope you paid him well. And you had my husband killed as well, because he won the deed to your property in a card game."

"She's crazy," said Fontaine. "I am an important member of the Las Vegas business community. Why would I welsh on a gambling debt?"

."You probably didn't," I said. "Your partner did that and was trying to get the property back before you found out. You're clever, but not clever enough." I was really getting wound up now. "Trusting this Fletcher person,"— I indicated the mug shot—"to do your dirty work was a big mistake. He doesn't have the brains for it. First he risks gambling your deed in a high-stakes poker game. Then he kills the wrong woman. And it was a real blunder to abduct Mr. and Mrs. Pickles. I'm sure the police will be adding that to your rap sheet."

Fontaine looked startled, as if finally realizing that I was more aware of what he'd been up to than he'd guessed.

"I figured out that's why you showed up at the ostrich ranch in such a hurry," I continued. "You were trying to head him off. Then he leaves clues all over the place leading us right to where he had them imprisoned at the Twilight Zone Motel. That's why you had them moved to the Big Top. You have a part interest there, and you're the casino vet, so no one would question it if they saw you bringing in a large, covered cage."

Fontaine was on his feet now. "Lies, all lies," he declared.

"I can prove every word is true," I said, being unfortunately inspired to add, "Clever clogs."

"Listen, ma'am," said Detective Davidson. "You're in a lot of trouble here, making these accusations. Where's your proof?"

I opened my mouth to speak, then closed it again abruptly. I was going to tell him what Punch had told me—how he suspected Roger had died that night—when I realized that I would be betraying the confidence of my clown friends.

"I'm not at liberty to say," I said quietly.

Mallory threw up his hands in frustration.

"You see. She's bluffing," said Fontaine. "Ask her why she killed Posey Brightman and took off immediately afterward."

Now he was trying to pin Posey's murder on me! Well, he wouldn't get away with that. I had plenty of witnesses who had seen me in Las Vegas at the time that Posey was killed.

Mallory took up the questioning. "Delilah, you're going to have to explain why you think a respected veterinarian like Dr. Fontaine would be harassing your friends over an ostrich ranch. And what business is it of yours, anyway?"

I explained how I had discovered that the two parcels of land, mine and the Pickles', were adjacent. I had reason to believe that silver had been discovered on both properties, and while Fontaine was determined to get back my parcel, which he considered rightfully his, by whatever means possible, the Pickles' parcel was a different matter. He had tried to scare them off, but they were not willing to sell.

By the time I finished, Dr. Leo Fontaine, veterinarian to the stars, was demanding that he be allowed to speak to his attorney.

"And where's this Lofty, alias Bud Fletcher, you keep talking about?" asked Mallory.

"He won't be hard to find," I said. "He's either in my car in the Big Top car park or at the nearest hospital. Just follow the trail of blood."

I felt a little ashamed about hiding the deed in the steel-jaw trap, set to snap shut as soon as anyone tried to remove it. But not too. After all Lofty had done much worse to Posey and Roger.

In the end, the charges against me were dropped, but not before I was informed I might be required to return to Las Vegas as a witness in Roger's murder trial. And, if charges were ever brought against the animal activists, I could be called as witness in that case, also. In that event, I would have to make sure I was out of the country at the time.

But there was still one mystery that remained to be solved.

♣ 22 ♣

Filling in the Blanks

"WHAT IN THE world was ailing Big Gus?" That was the question on Alf's mind that night when I met up with my friends again.

Evie and Howard had dropped me off at Judy's on the way to their suite at the Big Top. They had pressed me to go with them, but I was anxious to see how my other friends had fared after they had scarpered from the riot squad and, of course, I had to get Watson and see that Bertie and Trixie were okay. I still didn't know if Punch, Tony and the Pickles had made a clean getaway or run afoul of Lofty, who we now knew as Bud Fletcher, on their way out. The latter wasn't very likely, considering the trap I had set for him.

Mallory remained at the police station and appeared to be prepared to work through the night. Since two jurisdictions were involved in his case, that meant at least double the paperwork. He had offered to call me later, but the only telephone number I could have given him was Judy's, and I didn't want to be responsible for leading the police to the activists' home base.

At Judy's I had been greeted with open arms by Gert and Alf, who expressed their joy at finding Bertie safe and sound.

"Ee by gum, it's just grand to see him again. Thank you so much, Delilah, for taking such good care of him," one or the other of them repeated again and again.

Their delight was equalled only by Bertie's pleasure in seeing them, though he was somewhat less effusive, his demonstration limited to heavy tail thumping, head down for scratching, then rolling over on his back for a tummy rub. The three of them took up the entire couch, so I perched on the armrest while we talked.

When she could make her way through the bouncing poodles that greeted my arrival, Watson in her own, sweet, gentle manner came up and nuzzled my hand. Had she thought I'd abandoned her forever? Surely not. But how can they know, when we leave them at the groomer's, the vet's, or even with a friendly pet-sitter, that they will ever see us again? If we could only make them understand, I think the parting would at least be less wrenching for us, if not for them.

Judy had ordered pizza and several half-empty cardboard boxes lay on the coffee table.

"Here, Delilah, try this," said Tony, handing me a veggie slice. "I just heated it up in the microwave for you. Just like muvver used to make."

There was laughter all around.

Gert gave me a nudge. "Oh, that Tony, 'e's a caution," she said. " 'E's 'ad us in stitches ever since we got 'ere. And he really kept our spirits up when we was stuck in that cage."

I was delighted to see how well my friends were all getting along. The events that had brought them together seemed to have cemented a lasting friendship.

Over pizza and cups of hot chocolate—generously

laced with brandy from a bottle the larcenous Tony had nicked somewhere between the casino basement and Judy's place—I told them about my experiences at the police station, about how Mallory's investigation into Posey's murder had led him to Las Vegas, and what I had learned about Dr. Fontaine.

Gert and Alf were dismayed at how they'd been so taken in by their vet.

"To think that all the time he was treating our Big Gus he was trying to get 'is 'ands on our property," said Alf.

"Never mind, luv," said Gert. "We'll get it sorted all in good time." She gave him a hug. "Sup up yer cocoa."

Punch had been on the telephone arranging for the Pug's owners to pick up their pet. He was still wearing his tramp clown outfit.

"Mission accomplished," he said, when he put down the phone. "The owners will be here to pick up Romeo tomorrow."

I thanked him for orchestrating our brilliant and timely rescue. "Your timing was perfect. How did you do it? We,"—I indicated Alf, Gert and Tony—"didn't have any idea Dr. Fontaine was going to show up."

He smiled sheepishly. "Neither did I," he said. "It was pure chance."

We listened intently as he related how his attempt to rescue Romeo had been interrupted by an alert stagehand who had triggered the trapdoor at the opportune moment. "Fortunately, I already had tight hold of the dog," he finished.

Something still puzzled me. "Did you know Dr. Fontaine was Lofty's, aka Fletcher's, boss?" I asked him.

Punch nodded. "I knew they were operating a real estate scam together," he said. "But I didn't know they'd go so far as to murder someone to get what they wanted. Not until after the night Roger disappeared."

There was nothing to be gained by pointing out the obvious. That he should have gone to the police back then with his suspicions. I was quite sure he felt guilty enough about that already.

"Why do you think they waited for two years before renewing their search for the deed?" I asked him.

Punch thought for a moment, then said, "Best I can figure is, after they killed Roger they decided they'd better lie low for a bit. But lately, when Fontaine needed funds to increase his holding in the Big Top, he must have thought it was worth the risk to try to get his hands on the deed again. Then he got greedy, and decided to go for the adjacent property, too."

My friends were all eager to hear what had happened after they escaped from the casino basement, narrowly avoiding the riot squad coming in. They had not seen Evie and me taken away in the paddywagon. For all they knew, we might have once again become victims of Dr. Fontaine.

Then Alf, in his deliberate north country manner, told how he and Gert had been abducted from the ranch. "We were home, just putting the kettle on for a cuppa, when that Lofty bloke came storming into the house without so much as a by your leave. Threatening us, and demanding to know where you was, Delilah."

Here Gert chimed in. "He shoved us into that Corvette—lor' what a squeeze—and made us leave poor Bertie behind. Said there wasn't enough room. Wouldn't even let us take the time to shut him safely in the house. Just left him wandering around the yard with his lead on. Thank goodness you came along when you did, dearie."

She leaned over and patted my knee, then continued, "I told 'is nibs, I said, 'that Delilah will be along soon. She'll take care of our Bertie. She'll know what to do.' And, of course, you did. Mind you, we didn't let on to that Lofty chap that you was on your way. We were worried that he would come back and get you."

"I tried to warn you," I said. "They had found out somehow that I wasn't dead—that they'd killed the wrong person. But when Lofty arrived at the ranch and found that you, not me, had been driving my car, he must have decided that he would try and salvage the situation and please his boss at the same time by kidnapping you and forcing you to sell the property. When Fontaine got word of it, he hurried to the ranch, probably intent on stopping him, thinking the plan too risky. And that's when I met him."

"He must've nabbed you and yer missus just before I got there," Tony said to Alf. He put a near-empty pizza box on the floor for Trixie. Watson and Bertie looked on wistfully, but Trixie snuzzled the bits of leftover cheese and pepperoni, growling if they got too close. Bertie and Watson were too well trained to make an issue of it.

"When I saw the motor home arrive, I couldn't see who was driving it," Tony continued. "Then I saw Delilah's old banger in the driveway and wondered what the 'ell was going on. I thought I'd better keep a low profile until I could find out. Then, after the vet left and me and Delilah was 'aving a cup of cha in the kitchen, I saw the motel bookmatches and guessed that's where the trail led."

"I thought as much," I said. "I saw them, too."

Tony grinned. "You don't miss much, do you? I did try to 'ide 'em from you. Didn't want you getting into any more trouble. But you was too quick."

He paused and poured more brandy into his cup. "Any old 'ow, I checked into the motel and started snooping around, but before I got very far, old Lofty shows up, bops me over the noggin', and when I come to I found meself locked up in a cage like some bleedin' wild animal."

"Serves you right," I said, only half joking. "If you'd let me in on things from the beginning, we would've been able to look out for each other."

The sofa arm was getting uncomfortable, and I shifted my position. "But what were you doing in Vegas in the first place?" I said. "That's what I'd like to know. You never did tell me."

Trixie had finished the pizza crumbs and pawed at Tony's leg to be picked up. He obliged, and she snuggled down in his lap. "Well, I figured the less you knew, the better. But the fact of the matter is, I knew Punch, here"—he nodded in Punch's direction—"from the old days. We'd 'ung out together with your old man, Roger, in Las Vegas, and of course we was all together at the card game that night you showed up looking for a lost dog."

He took a swig of his hot chocolate and brandy and smacked his lips. "Well, after your house was broken into the other day"—was it really just the other day? It seemed like weeks since I'd left home—"I got a phone call from Punch, 'ere. Said that he'd 'eard Lofty was suspicious that since Roger didn't 'ave the deed on 'im, and 'e couldn't find it at your house, then maybe Roger'd slipped it to me, and that's why I'd left the card game early. Said they might be coming after me next."

He stroked Trixie's ear absently and was rewarded with an enthusiastic face-licking. "Give over, luv," he said affectionately, then continued. "That's when I decided to come to Las Vegas to get it sorted. I came over to ask you to take care of Trixie for me while I was gone, but you was all for going to Vegas yourself."

I moved from the sofa arm and sat on the floor with my back resting against the sofa's end and petted Watson, who lay down alongside. "What I'd like to know was how Lofty knew that he'd killed the wrong person, and that I was still alive," I said. "The people at the Lucky Hitch didn't know my name. I left a message on Posey's machine, but she was probably already dead by then. The only other person I met after that was Mort Falco, the attorney. But my name wouldn't mean anything to him, unless—"

"Unless he was in on it," said Alf. "Come to think on it, it was Dr. Fontaine who referred us to Falco, and Falco advised us to sell out that day we went to see him."

"So," put in Judy, serving another round of hot chocolate, "probably as soon as Delilah left his office he was on the phone to Bud Fletcher." She grinned and looked across at me. "Sorry, Lofty to you."

"We're thinking of selling the property anyway," said Alf, pouring more brandy into his and Gert's cups, then holding it over my cup. I shook my head—I was beginning to feel a little squiffy—and Alf continued. "With Big Gus doing so poorly, like, maybe it's just not meant to be. He's just not thriving."

Just then Harry, the computer man, emerged from his alcove and slipped a piece of paper into my hand. On it he had written "Deiffenbachia, poisonous. Chopped up leaves will make animal sick for a few hours. Symptoms: lethargy, vomiting; slowly causes paralysis of vocal cords, difficulty in eating, swallowing."

"Thanks, Harry," I said. "Won't you join us?" But Harry seemed only to need the companionship of his chat room pals. He shook his head, helped himself to a slice of cold pizza, and shuffled back to his computer.

"I think this, or something similar, is what's been ailing Big Gus," I said, passing the paper to Alf.

I told them about the potted plants in the back of Dr. Fontaine's Range Rover. "My guess is he'd been feeding Big Gus poisonous plants. Not enough to kill him, mind you, but enough to keep making him sick."

"Well, I never," declared Gert. "You really are a pet detective, aren't you! But now you mention it, I always wondered why he had all them plants in his car. And to think that all along we was paying that sod good money to find out what the problem was."

Tony got up and stretched. I think I'll take the dogs for a walk," he said, opening the door to the back yard. "Looks like none of us are going to get any kip tonight, anyway. "Sun's coming up."

"Good heavens!" I said, glancing at my watch. It was nearly five o'clock. It had been a long night, and we'd stayed up talking until dawn. Just as well. There was no way Judy could have provided us all with sleeping accommodation.

I helped her tidy up the place while Gert did the dishes.

Alf, who had been dozing on the sofa, roused and got on the telephone to arrange for a rental car to take them back to the ranch. All too soon we were saying our good-byes. Gert thanked me once again for "saving our Bertie," adding her appreciation for discovering what was ailing Big Gus. She was anxious to get home to see how he was faring.

"He was fine when we left," I said, telling her how he had chased Trixie around the paddock. "Of course, Dr. Fontaine did say he'd send his assistant over to feed them." Seeing the alarm on Gert's face, I hastily added, "But my guess is he had too much else on his mind to remember to do so."

I had grown very fond of this couple. I don't think they ever quite realized just how close to death they'd come. But I was glad they had emerged from the ordeal with their wonderful optimism still in tact. Tears filled my eyes as we said good-bye.

"Best be off then," Gert said with a sigh when their rental car arrived. "Ee, by gum, it's been lovely to see you again, Delilah, luv. Promise you'll come and visit us again soon. You need fattening up with some good English cooking."

"Aye," added her husband. "You just watch you don't fall down no grating."

I summoned a smile, as I leaned down to hug Bertie.

Chuckling, Gert gave me one last hug, kissed Watson on the head, and they were gone.

I felt almost as tearful saying good-bye to Punch and Judy—I never did discover their real names. We had become good friends in such a brief period of time. Several months later I learned that Punch had turned state's evidence during Roger's murder trial. As a result, he and Judy went into the witness protection program—from where I'm sure they will continue their animal rights activities. Whenever I hear of any demonstrations, I think of them and wonder.

Tony and I shared a cab to pick up our cars. "Can't wait to get the 'ell out of this place," he said with feeling, when I dropped him and Trixie off at the Twilight Zone Motel. "The waves are calling me. See you back in Surf City, luv."

I waved good-bye and told the taxi driver to take me to the Big Top parking lot. I hoped my car would still be there.

It was. And leaning against it was Jack Mallory.

· 23 ·

Second Thoughts

WATSON BOUNDED OUT of the taxi and, by the time I'd paid the driver, Mallory had her jumping up in anticipation of the treat he'd brought for her.

"I was hoping you'd give me a ride back to Surf City," he said as I joined them.

He looked remarkably relaxed for someone who'd been working all night. Maybe it was the jeans and freshly laundered dark blue shirt. He'd obviously put more thought into packing for a short trip out of town than I had.

I wondered, since he was on expenses, why he didn't fly back. Surely much more convenient. Could it be that he might like my company?

He must have sensed my hesitation. "Would you like me to drive?"

That clinched it. I had not been looking forward to the long journey alone. I smiled. "I'd be glad of your company."

I had expected Evie to come with me, but she was determined to stay in Las Vegas with Howard until he concluded his business deal.

"I intend to stay right here until he has divested himself of his share in that dreadful Big Top," she'd said when she'd kissed me good-bye the previous night. "I'm trying to persuade him to put the money into something closer to home. A nice little dress shop would do very well. Or, even better, a jewelry store." She giggled at the thought.

"Sorry the RNM turned out to be such a dud," she continued. "But that detective of yours is really very fond of you. I was watching him back there at the police station. Concern written all over his face." She paused before adding. "You could do worse."

Though still roadworthy, the interior of my car was a complete mess, having been thoroughly turned over by Lofty not once but twice in the course of the last few days. The cardboard box containing the steel-jawed trap was no longer there. It had been removed, along with the wounded Lofty, by the LVPD during the night, Mallory explained.

The front bench seat had been ripped open to expose the springs. I padded it as best I could with Watson's blanket, but it did not promise to be a comfortable ride.

Like the car, I looked decidedly the worse for wear. After a quick shower at Judy's house I had donned the shorts and T-shirt I'd laundered at the RV park. Clean, but somewhat rumpled from being stuffed into the carryall. My nose was raw from the red clown proboscis, my hair still damp. I looked for all the world like an angry cat, I decided, taking a quick glance in the vanity mirror.

Watson fidgeted in the back. Without her blankie, she was having trouble finding a comfortable spot. Finally, she settled down with a deep sigh and a glare in my direction. She knew where that blanket was.

After we got underway, Mallory concentrated on the road, coaxing more speed out of the old banger than I'd ever been able to. He seemed to be brooding about something. I guessed he was disgusted with me for ignoring him when he'd advised me against going to Las Vegas by myself.

Well, if he was waiting for an apology he'd better not hold his breath.

We travelled in silence for almost an hour. Then we both turned to speak at the same time.

"If it's about—"

"You first," he said.

"No," I said. "Go ahead. You've obviously got something on your mind. We've got plenty of time."

"Just wanted to say how sorry I am about your husband."

"You didn't even know him. Why should you be sorry?" And why did I have to be so ungracious? "Besides, from what we've learned, it sounds like he got what he deserved. You're probably thinking that the world's well rid of Roger Doolittle."

"He was your husband."

"For about six months. And I'm a complete idiot for trusting him."

"But you must have cared for him."

"Of course I cared for him. I married him, didn't I? You must think me a very poor judge of character."

But Mallory evidently thought no such thing. He sighed. "You seem determined to misunderstand me, Delilah."

We travelled on for a few more miles before he spoke again.

"I really wonder about you, Delilah. Why you have this compulsion to ignore the professionals and take so many risks. You've been dealing with a really bad bunch this time."

"I suppose you'd have preferred that I stayed home and got myself killed instead?" I fidgeted in my seat trying to avoid the protruding springs. "I'm sorry. It must be the heat that's making me so disagreeable. You're right, I should have listened to you, and I—"

"No, don't promise that you'll act differently in the future. I know that the next time there's an animal in trouble, you'll go tearing off without thinking of—of anybody else. Your friends, I mean."

"Actually, I wasn't going to say any such thing," I said, rattled. "I was going to say how very provoking you are, always being so right."

Apart from a brief stop to stretch our legs and have a cup of coffee, we drove straight through. Neither of us were inclined to be obliged to make polite conversation over an indifferent hamburger at some tourist trap.

The cool air blowing in from the ocean as we neared Surf City was a welcome relief from the dry desert heat of the last few days.

It was strange coming home to a house that had so recently been the scene of a brutal murder.

The first thing I noticed when we approached the front door was that the broken stained glass window insert had been replaced. Not with a pelican, but with a hummingbird, hovering over a pink hibiscus.

I gasped when I saw it.

"Couldn't find a pelican," said Mallory, almost apologetically. "Not in time, anyway. And I wanted it fixed before you got back."

"You did this?" I said in surprisc. "It's quite lovely. And it's so very kind of you to take the trouble."

"A pleasure," he said. We both went to pass through the front door at the same time, and he took the opportunity to give me a quick hug. "I wanted to make your homecoming as pleasant as possible."

There were other reminders of the recent past. Someone, probably the police, had moved the furniture around. A faint smell of Lysol hung in the air as if someone—Ariel perhaps—had been cleaning. A roughly boarded up front window was presumably the one that had been smashed after Evie had looked in and seen what she thought was my body lying on the floor. I felt another pang as I imagined her distress.

As soon as we entered the sitting room, Watson started to sniff at the bloodstained carpet.

Mallory uttered a grunt of annoyance. "They were supposed to pick that up and have it dry-cleaned before you got back," he said.

"How thoughtful. I didn't know the police did things like that."

"They don't, usually," he said. I guessed it was something else he had taken upon himself to do. He was really an extraordinarily kind man.

Ariel had obviously got my message and come in and cared for Dolly-bird and Hobo. Their dishes were full of fresh food and water. I opened a new bag of kibble and shook some into Watson's empty dish, and poured fresh water into her bowl.

I put the kettle on. I'd been looking forward to a cup

of tea ever since we'd left Las Vegas, even before. My last good cuppa had been at the ostrich ranch, and I was suffering severe withdrawal symptoms.

Mallory showed no sign of leaving. And, as if in anticipation of him staying awhile, Watson ran and got her sock rope and laid it at his feet.

"Now, Watson," I said. "He doesn't have time to play with you. He has to get home."

Mallory tugged at the rope absently for a moment or two, then said, "I suppose I'd better call someone for a ride."

"Oh, sorry. Of course. You should have said something. I could have dropped you off."

But he knew that. He must have wanted to come in.

"Can I offer you something to eat?" I asked. "Not that I've got much in." I opened the pantry door and looked in hopefully, as if maybe the food fairies had replenished it during my absence. I hadn't yet replaced the staples spoiled by the break-in.

"I suppose I could microwave something," I said, as if to do so would be a most unusual occurrence, though it certainly was nothing of the sort.

"What have you got?"

I opened the refrigerator and surveyed the contents. A few doubtful eggs, probably past their pull date. In the freezer, some stale bread and staler cheese.

"Not much here," I said forlornly.

Mallory looked in the pantry. "What do you mean? You've got all kinds of stuff." He brought forth a jar of salsa, a box of muffin mix, and a packet of dates.

"Why don't you sit down and have your tea while I fix something?"

"Gladly," I said, though horrified to imagine what combination he might make of his foraging. "It's all yours."

While Mallory busied himself in the kitchen, I took my tea into the bathroom and ran myself a hot shower. After blow-drying my hair, I stepped into a sage-green terry jumpsuit. It was the only thing I could find that was clean, and I knew that the colour was becoming.

The smell of something delicious cooking made my mouth water. I returned to the kitchen to find the table set for two and a fresh pot of tea on the stove. With a policeman's powers of observation, Mallory must have watched how I had made it.

"Sit down," he commanded, looking very pleased with himself as he placed before me a plate of a light-as-air cheese and salsa omelette and warm date muffins.

I don't know if it was the company or the food; more likely it was because I was so tired and hungry I would have appreciated anything that I didn't have to fix myself, but it was quite the most delicious meal I had ever tasted.

"I didn't know you could cook," I said.

"There's a lot about me you don't know. How do you think I manage, living by myself? I don't like to eat out all the time. But it's nice to have someone to share it with. This is something we should do more of." He gave me a meaningful glance.

"You're right. And we shall," I promised. After all, the man had possibilities. As Evie had said, I could do worse. Much worse.

Clearly the time had come to let go of Roger's ghost and put the past to rest. Any new relationship would, of course, depend on whether or not Watson was allowed to sleep on the bed.